Deformed

WARRIORS
FIELD GUIDE

WARRIORS

Book One: Into the Wild

Book Two: Fire and Ice

Book Three: Forest of Secrets

Book Four: Rising Storm

Book Five: A Dangerous Path

Book Six: The Darkest Hour

WARRIORS: THE NEW PROPHECY

Book One: Midnight

Book Two: Moonrise

Book Three: Dawn

Book Four: Starlight

Book Five: Twilight

Book Six: Sunset

WARRIORS: POWER OF THREE

Book One: The Sight

WARRIORS (MANGA):

The Lost Warrior

WARRIORS FIELD GUIDE: Secrets of the Clans

WARRIORS
FIELD GUIDE

SECRETS
OF THE
CLANS

ERIN HUNTER
ILLUSTRATED *by* WAYNE McLOUGHLIN

HarperCollins*Publishers*

Special thanks to
Tui Sutherland

For Cyd, because she loves cats, and for Rebekah,
because I'm sure she will, too.

Warriors Field Guide: Secrets of the Clans
Text copyright © 2007 by Working Partners Limited
Illustrations copyright © 2007 by Wayne McLoughlin
Series created by Working Partners Limited
All rights reserved. Printed in China.
No part of this book may be used or reproduced in any manner whatsoever
without written permission except in the case of brief quotations embodied
in critical articles and reviews. For information address
HarperCollins Children's Books,
a division of HarperCollins Publishers,
10 East 53rd Street, New York, NY 10022.
www.harpercollinschildrens.com

Library of Congress Cataloging-in-Publication Data
Hunter, Erin.
    Warriors field guide : secrets of the clans / Erin Hunter. —1st ed.
        p.   cm. — (Warriors)
    Summary: Provides background information about the history, characters, and places of
significance to the warrior cats featured in the series Warriors and Warriors, the new prophecy.
    Contents: Thunder, Wind, River, Shadow, and Star: the Clans — Territories: homes and
hunting grounds — Cats outside the Clans: Kittypets, Rogues, and others — Other animals:
animals to hunt, fight, fear, and respect — The Warrior Code: the principles a warrior must
live by — Ceremonies: how a warrior becomes a leader — Prophecies and omens: foretelling
the future — Medicine: healing the Clans — Mythology: LionClan, TigerClan, LeopardClan.
    ISBN-13: 978-0-06-123903-8 (trade bdg.) — ISBN-10: 0-06-123903-8 (trade bdg.)
    ISBN-13: 978-0-06-123904-5 (lib. bdg.) — ISBN-10: 0-06-123904-6 (lib. bdg.)
    [1. Cats—Fiction.   2. Fantasy.]   I. Hunter, Erin. Warriors.   II. Hunter, Erin. Warriors,
the new prophecy.   III. Title.
PZ7.H916625War 2007   2006036237
[Fic]—dc22

Typography by Larissa Lawrynenko

First Edition
12 13 SCP 20 19 18 17 16 15 14

CONTENTS

THUNDER, WIND, RIVER, SHADOW, AND STAR:

THE CLANS

*The story of the beginning of the warrior Clans
has been passed down by cats of all Clans, from elder to warrior,
from warrior to apprentice, from queen to kit. The story
is never the same twice, and parts grow uncertain,
or they become suddenly clear in the telling. There are some cats
who walk dimly, their names and deeds lost in the sweet fog
of the elders' den, for the warrior Clans have roamed
the forest for moons beyond counting. . . .*

WARRIORS FIELD GUIDE

HISTORY OF THE GLANS

Many moons ago, the forest was a wilderness, untamed by territories. In the north lay sweeping moorland; in the south was dense woodland. On the edge of the trees, a tumbling river flowed out of a dark ravine.

Cats came into the forest. They were drawn by the soft rustlings of small creatures, shadows under the water, and the sudden commotion of birds' wings in the trees. These were not warrior cats. They lived in small groups, not yet Clans. There were no borders set down. And they fought constantly, fearful that prey might run out and that their overlapping territories were being threatened. It was a lawless, bloody time for the forest, and many cats died.

One night, when the moon was full, the cats agreed to meet at a clearing in the forest surrounded by four great oak trees. They argued over stolen prey. Claws flashed; challenging yowls rang across the forest. A terrible battle followed, and soon the ground was wet with spilled blood.

Many cats died that night. Exhausted by their wounds, the survivors slept where they had fought. When they woke they were bathed in moonlight. All around them they saw the spirits of their slain kin, no longer torn and bloodied but shining like fallen stars. They huddled on the ground, and, as the spirits spoke, they saw terrible visions of the future. They saw the forest drowned in blood, their kits stalked by death at every pawstep. And they knew that the fighting had to end.

"Unite or die," said the spirits.

From among the living cats, a black female was the first to speak. She rose from the ground on stiff, battle-wearied legs. "My name is Shadow," she mewed. "How should we unite, unless we have a leader? I can hunt in the depths of the darkest night. Let Shadow rule the forest!"

"And you would lead us into darkness too!" meowed a silvery gray tom with green eyes. "I am River! I move through the forest along secret paths and hidden places. It is River, not Shadow, who should unite the forest!"

"The forest is more than River and Shadow," growled a wiry brown female. "Wind alone reaches its distant corners. I am as fast as the wind that blows from the high moors. *I* should be the ruler."

The largest surviving cat was called Thunder. He was a fiery orange tom with amber eyes and large white paws. "What good is any of that compared to my strength and skill at hunting? If any cat was born to rule, it is I."

A furious yowling broke out under the four great oaks, watched in silence by the spirit-cats. Dark clouds suddenly blew across the moon, and the living cats trembled in fear. On the top of a high rock, they saw a tabby cat, one of the fallen, her fur shining though there was no light in the sky. Her eyes flashed angrily at the cats on the ground.

"You are all as foolish as ducks!" she meowed. "Can't you think beyond yourselves for one moment? Think of your kits!"

The four cats—Shadow, River, Wind, and Thunder—looked up at the tabby, but none of them spoke.

"The forest is big enough to feed all your families and many more," she meowed. "You must find other cats like you, choose a home in the forest, and set down borders."

At that moment, the moon broke free of the clouds, revealing a circle of starlit spirit-cats around the edge of the clearing. A white tom stepped forward. "If you do this," he meowed, "we will reward you with eight more lives, so that you may lead your Clans for many moons to come."

Next to speak was a slender tortoiseshell. She stepped forward and stood beside the white tom. "We will watch over you from Silverpelt," she promised, and lifted her eyes to the crowded path of stars that swept across the night sky. "We will visit you in your dreams and guide you on your journeys."

"Once a month," meowed the white tom, "at the full moon, you will gather together here, between the four great oak trees, for a night of truce. You will see us above you in Silverpelt and know we are watching. And if blood is spilled on those nights, you will know we are angry."

"You will be warriors!" yowled the tabby from the high rock.

Thunder, River, Wind, and Shadow bowed their heads.

"From now on, you will live by a warrior code. Your hearts will be filled with courage and nobility, and if you must fight, it will be not for greed, but for honor and justice."

There was a long silence. Finally Thunder nodded his broad orange head. "This is wise advice. I believe we can choose our territories and lay down borders fairly, in peace."

One by one, the other cats murmured their agreement. Then they returned to their homes and sought out cats like themselves, with similar strengths and abilities. River found cats willing to fish for their prey. Shadow gathered nighttime hunters with clever minds and sharp claws. Thunder found hunters who could track prey through the thickest undergrowth. To Wind came the fastest runners and cats who loved the open moors. Then they divided the forest so each Clan had enough prey to survive, and all the cats could live in safety. And when the leaders returned to the four great oaks for the first night of the full-moon truce, their starry ancestors gave them eight more lives, as they had promised.

There was not always peace between the Clans, but that was to be expected—cats are born with claws and teeth for a reason. Still, as long as they lived by the warrior code, their fallen ancestors would watch over them and guide them through their lives.

And so the age of the warrior Clans began.

THE WARRIOR CODE

1. Defend your Clan, even with your life. You may have friendships with cats from other Clans, but your loyalty must remain to your Clan, as one day you may meet them in battle.

2. Do not hunt or trespass on another Clan's territory.

3. Elders and kits must be fed before apprentices and warriors. Unless they have permission, apprentices may not eat until they have hunted to feed the elders.

4. Prey is killed only to be eaten. Give thanks to StarClan for its life.

5. A kit must be at least six moons old to become an apprentice.

6. Newly appointed warriors will keep a silent vigil for one night after receiving their warrior name.

7. A cat cannot be made deputy without having mentored at least one apprentice.

8. The deputy will become Clan leader when the leader dies or retires.

9. After the death or retirement of the deputy, the new deputy must be chosen before moonhigh.

10. A gathering of all four Clans is held at the full moon during a truce that lasts for the night. There shall be no fighting among Clans at this time.

11. Boundaries must be checked and marked daily. Challenge all trespassing cats.

12. No warrior may neglect a kit in pain or in danger, even if that kit is from a different Clan.

13. The word of the Clan leader is the warrior code.

14. An honorable warrior does not need to kill other cats to win his battles, unless they are outside the warrior code or it is necessary for self-defense.

15. A warrior rejects the soft life of a kittypet.

THUNDERCLAN

FIRESTAR ON THUNDERCLAN

I am Firestar. Welcome to ThunderClan—the
Clan of courage and loyalty. I was not a forest-born cat, but
ThunderClan welcomed me, and once I proved myself
as a warrior, they grew to respect me. I have risen to become
their leader and I would lay down all nine of my lives
for my Clan, just as my Clanmates would lay down their lives
for me and for each other. There is no other Clan in
the forest so true or so brave. I respect and admire the other
Clans, but my heart is here, with ThunderClan—
the Clan of heroes, the Clan of compassion,
the Clan of destiny.

> **Clan character:** In peace, respectful of other Clans. In battle, fierce, courageous, and loyal. ThunderClan cats speak out for what is right and are not afraid to challenge the warrior code.
>
> **Prey:** Mice, voles, squirrels, the occasional rabbit, and birds such as starlings, magpies, wood pigeons, and thrushes.
>
> **Hunting skills:** Excellent stalking techniques. They keep upwind of their prey, creeping across the forest floor unseen and unheard.

THUNDERCLAN FOREST TERRITORY

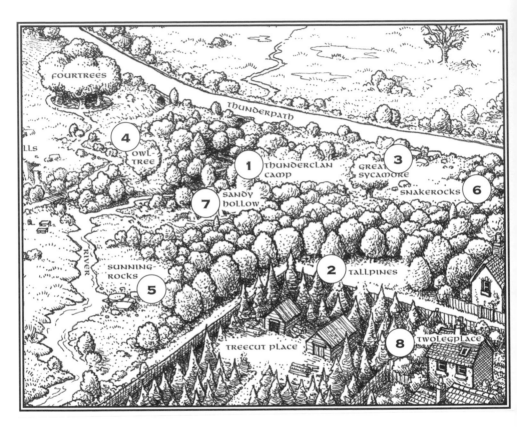

(1) **ThunderClan camp:** Sheltered at the foot of a sandy ravine and well protected by thornbushes, this camp is hard to attack and easy to defend.

(2) **Tallpines:** Watch out for the Twoleg tree-eater! It makes the ground rumble and leaves deep gullies that fill with muddy water.

(3) **Great Sycamore:** Its branches are thick and strong all the way to the ends. Young apprentices learn to climb here and dare one another to climb higher.

(4) Owl-Tree: Halfway up the trunk is a hole that is home to a tawny owl that flies out at night. Legend has it that an early ThunderClan apprentice learned the secrets of night hunting from one such owl. Every night, as the moon rose, he would wait at the foot of the Owl-Tree. When the owl swooped out, he followed, like the owl's shadow cast by the moon on the ground. Eventually this bold young apprentice became a great leader known as Owlstar. In the hunt, he was as silent and deadly as the tawny owl.

(5) Sunningrocks: A warm spot in the sunshine. Keep a sharp eye out for prey darting between the cracks! Many moons ago, when the river was much wider than it is now, Sunningrocks was an island. Only RiverClan cats could swim out to it. Then the water dropped, and Sunningrocks became part of the forest shore, so ThunderClan claimed it. They did not allow RiverClan cats to cross their territory to reach it. Since then, many battles have been fought between the two Clans over these smooth, sun-warmed stones.

(6) Snakerocks: Beware poisonous adders! Chervil grows abundantly here. The caves beneath the rocks provide shelter for dangerous animals, like foxes, badgers—and even dogs.

(7) Sandy hollow: A training hollow surrounded by trees. Warrior apprentices are unlikely to hurt themselves on the soft ground.

(8) Twolegplace: A maze of small Thunderpaths and Twoleg dens (see *Other Animals, Twolegs*). There are two different kinds of cats in Twolegplace: loners and kittypets (see *Cats Outside the Clans, Rogues and Loners,* and *Kittypets*).

BRIGHTHEART SPEAKS:
The Death of Swiftpaw

It wasn't fair that only Cloudpaw got to be a warrior. We were just as good and we tried so hard, but Bluestar ignored us and treated us like dopey kits.

Swiftpaw said we should do something so brave that Bluestar would have to make us warriors too. None of us knew what had been eating the prey around Snakerocks, but Swiftpaw figured if we went out there, we'd find a trail to follow. It made sense, you know? We'd follow the trail, find out who was stealing our prey, and then come back to tell Bluestar. And then we'd be warriors!

Swiftpaw knew a way out through the ferns behind the elders' den, so we sneaked out just before dawn and headed for Snakerocks. My paws trembled as we raced through the leaves. I knew my mentor, Whitestorm, would be angry with me—apprentices are not supposed to leave the camp without permission. But he'd be impressed when I helped save the Clan!

The smell near Snakerocks was strange—fierce and dark. I slowed down, but Swiftpaw kept running.

"Swiftpaw!" I hissed as he scrambled over a fallen tree. "Be careful!"

"Don't worry!" he called back. "There's nothing here!"

Just as he said that, a huge shape flew out of the cave and

fastened slavering jaws around Swiftpaw's throat. It was a dog—the largest I'd ever seen. I wanted to run away more than I've ever wanted anything, but I couldn't leave Swiftpaw behind.

Swiftpaw wrenched himself around, snarling and twisting, but the dog shook him like he was a squirrel, and then threw him to the other side of the clearing. I ran over and saw that he was bleeding, but he managed to stand, turn, and fight. The dog came toward us, its head low, its teeth bared and gleaming. I crouched, waiting until it was a mouse-length away, and then I lashed out and raked my claws across its face. It jumped back with a yelp, and for a moment I thought, *We'll be okay. It's just one dog, and there're two of us.*

And then I saw the others.

There were at least six dogs ranged across the clearing, all of them four times our size or bigger. They growled so loud it felt like the earth was shaking. *"Pack, pack,"* they snarled. *"Kill, kill."*

And then they sprang. I darted forward, jumped up, and sank my claws into soft underbelly. As I clung on, scratching and biting, I could hear Swiftpaw—spitting, hissing, and yowling in rage and

defiance. The world turned upside down, and the air was knocked out of me. I remember dust, a forest of legs, flying fur, blood. At one point I saw Swiftpaw break free from the pack and climb a tree. I prayed to StarClan that he would make it, but huge paws brought him crashing to the ground. Then blood filled my eyes, and I saw no more. I could still hear, though—and in among the growling and snarling, there were yelps too. I don't know when the end came for Swiftpaw. I only remember him fighting like all of LionClan. That's how I will always remember him.

Then I was shaken loose. I felt light as air. I slammed against rock, and everything went dark.

I woke up in Cinderpelt's cave three sunrises later. Fireheart and Cloudtail had found me and brought me home. Cinderpelt said I had nightmares, calling out *"pack"* and *"kill"* in my sleep, but I can't remember any of them now.

The first thing I remember was the feeling of Cloudtail's warm white fur pressed against mine. When I moved, he woke up instantly, as if he'd been waiting the whole time for me to awaken.

I knew something was wrong right away. It wasn't just the pain—my face felt frozen, and I couldn't see anything on one side. I had lost an eye! When I saw what the dogs had done to me, I wished I had died fighting beside Swiftpaw. And when Bluestar gave me my warrior name, Lostface, I no longer knew who I was.

I would not have survived that dark time if it weren't for Cloudtail. He gave me another destiny, and I knew that no matter what I looked like, I would be all right. As long as Cloudtail loved me, I was no longer Lostface, but Brightheart.

THUNDERCLAN FOREST CAMP

Welcome to ThunderClan's forest camp! I'm Sandstorm, a ThunderClan warrior. Firestar has asked me to show you around. Watch out, though. Some of the elders might be cranky if we disturb them while they're having a nap.

Can you see the camp entrance? Well hidden, isn't it? Those brambles protect us from predators, but they don't stop the sunshine from warming up the camp.

Follow me down the ravine. Bluestar says it used to be a river a long time ago, but I can't imagine that. It's so dry and sandy now. Keep your head down—we're going through this tunnel in the gorse. See the path under your paws? Hundreds of ThunderClan cats have been this way over many generations. Watch out for the prickles!

And here we are! No, Squirrelpaw, this is my guest. They didn't sneak up behind me. Yes, I know you're standing guard. I'm sure the whole camp knows we're here now.

Over this way is the nursery. See the thick bramble walls? The nursery is the strongest part of the Clan camp. Can you hear the kits mewing and playing inside? Queens and warriors will fight like TigerClan to protect them.

Notice the clump of ferns beside the tree stump? That's where the apprentices sleep. It's supposed to be lined with moss, but it looks like a certain apprentice has kicked up a bit of a mess. After guard duty, I promise you she will be cleaning it up. Poor Squirrelpaw! She has always been such a restless sleeper.

Warriors sleep under that bush—you can see the entrance tunnel there. As a senior warrior, I sleep in the center of the group, where it's warmest. I remember being a young warrior, though. It can get cold on the edge during leaf-bare!

This fallen tree is the elders' den. Go ahead, poke your nose inside. Oh, sorry, Dappletail! I'm giving a tour. No, they are not spying for ShadowClan! Don't you have an apprentice to torment, Dappletail?

Quickly, while she's gone, put your paws on the den floor. Don't the grass and moss feel soft? The apprentices keep it fresh. Nobody wants grumpy elders . . . well, no grumpier than usual.

Let's cross the clearing to that tall, smooth boulder over there. This is Highrock, and it's where our leader stands to make announcements to the whole Clan and to lead ceremonies. Can you picture it? You'd listen, wouldn't you?

Around here is Firestar's den. Hello? Firestar? He must be out on patrol. Peek through the lichen hanging over the entrance. This is where he sleeps. Before him it was Bluestar, and after him, who knows? Firepaw was a pudgy little kittypet when I first met him. Who could ever have dreamed he'd be our leader?

Before you go, let me show you the medicine cat's den. Come inside. I love the smell of the herbs. Leafpaw! That's my other daughter—she's in training to be a medicine cat, and she's very clever. She sleeps at this end of the fern tunnel. Her mentor, Cinderpelt, sleeps in that hole in the rock over there. Leafpaw! There you are. Always sorting herbs! She's so dedicated and hard-working. It makes me very proud.

What's that? You think your sister would rather be hunting than on guard duty? All right, I'll have a word with Firestar and see if she can come to the Gathering tonight—that should cheer her up.

And that's our camp! I should really be off hunting now. Watch your fur on the way out. And don't tell anyone you were here!

THUNDERCLAN LAKE
TERRITORY

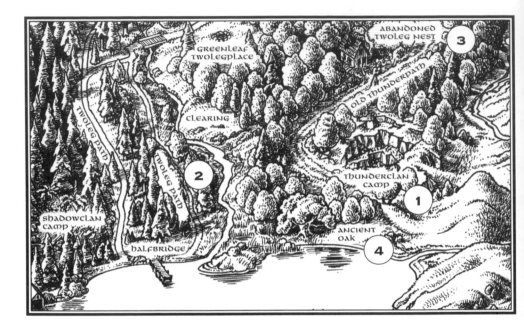

(1) ThunderClan camp: This symmetrical stone hollow, enclosed by towering cliffs of sheer stone left behind by Twolegs, was the obvious choice for ThunderClan's new camp.

(2) Twoleg paths: Twolegs mark their paths with shiny blue markers!

(3) Abandoned Twoleg nest: A good place for prey and an excellent source of herbs (see *Medicine, Catmint,* and *Borage Leaves*). It has an ominous, empty feeling and seems ready to fall down at any moment.

(4) Ancient Oak: In an old rabbit burrow below the twisting roots, Brambleclaw, Mistyfoot, Crowfeather, Tawnypelt, and Squirrelpaw sheltered on their first trip around the lake, scouting for new Clan territories and camps. Also known as Sky Oak.

THUNDERCLAN LAKE CAMP

hi! I'm Squirrelflight. I'm going to show you our new camp by the lake! It's perfect, and you know what? *I found it!*

I'll show you how I did it. Let's creep through these thorn-bushes here . . . okay, stop! Careful! You nearly did what I did, didn't you? Only I was running really fast after a vole. And suddenly—WHOMP! I took off through the air! And then I landed in a pile of brambles! Here, lie on your belly and peek over the edge of the cliff. See that bush down there? That's where I landed. Ouch!

But actually, I was lucky. If I'd tripped over that side instead, I would have had much farther to fall. These walls around the camp are tall and stone and hard to climb. Here, slide along this wall. Completely smooth, right? Isn't that weird? We think Twolegs were here a long time ago, slicing stone off the walls with their monsters. Don't ask me why! Twolegs are so mouse-brained.

Luckily they've gone away, and now there are lots of bushes and trees growing up over this hollow to protect us. The stone walls keep out the wind, although we have to watch our step near the edge. Brambleclaw keeps lecturing me about that. You'd think I was a newborn kit the way he talks to me!

All right, duck your head and squeeze through this thorn barrier. Intimidating, isn't it? If you were a ShadowClan cat, you'd probably turn tail rather than attack, wouldn't you?

Behold our beautiful camp! Isn't it amazing? Isn't it perfect? Did I mention that I found it? You've come at a good time—it's sunhigh, so lots of cats are sleeping. Look at grumpy old Mousefur over there, snoring away. The cat next to her with his nose in the air is Longtail. He's blind, but he can probably smell you; that's why he looks anxious. Don't be offended. Not every cat smells as great as ThunderClan.

Jump up on these rocks here—watch your claws; the rocks can be slippery. Now we're standing on the Highledge. You can see the whole camp! Firestar makes his announcements from up here. He puffs out his chest like this, and he struts forward like this, and then he opens his mouth and yowls: "Let all those cats old enough to catch their own prey join—"

Uh-oh. I think I did that a bit louder than I meant to. Here come Cloudtail, Dustpelt, and Brambleclaw. Quick, into Firestar's den! Oh, come on, move your fur, it's just a cave. In, in, in!

Isn't it cool in here? It's so dim and shady. Firestar sleeps back here on this bed of ferns and moss. It looks soft and springy. I

don't know how he keeps it so neat all the time. Doesn't it make you want to jump on it and roll around? Oops! I thought it would hold up better than that. Do you think he'll notice? Maybe we should get out of here.

See the caves where the apprentices and the elders sleep? The warriors—like me!—sleep under that big thornbush over there. Under the biggest bramble thicket is the nursery. Want to visit my friend Sorreltail? She has the cutest kits in the world. Come on, let's go over and stick our noses in.

Hello, Sorreltail. Hi, kittens! Oh, Sorreltail does look sleepy. Sorry, we'll let you get back to napping.

Across the camp is the medicine cat's den. Hurry, Brambleclaw is coming with his extra-grumpy face on. What cute kits! I don't want any of my own yet, though. I want to do a lot more warrior stuff first. Although it does look comfortable in the nursery.

You can't see the den here because it's hidden by this curtain of hanging bramble tendrils. But slip through it and—see? Look at this great cave! Hey, Leafpool, how's it going? My sister is our medicine cat. The smell in here always makes me sneeze. *Achoo!* Oops, sorry, Leafpool . . . were those supposed to be stacked like that? Look, this is my friend. I wanted to show how nice it is in here. It almost makes you want to get sick. The sand is really soft, and there's a little pool in the back for water. Leafpool stores her herbs in these cracks in the wall, or, I guess, out here in a pile where any cat can step on them. What? I didn't do it on purpose!

Uh-oh—hear that yowling? That's our bossy tabby friend looking for me. Perhaps you'd better go. Tell you what, I'll jump on him, and you make a dash for the tunnel. Then you *might* want to keep running as far and as fast as you can. Brambleclaw can be very serious about scaring off trespassers. Okay, ready? All right, go! Run! Quick as you can!

SIGNIFICANT LEADERS

Only some leaders and medicine cats are remembered by the Clans. Their names cast long shadows over the history of the forest; their deeds—good or evil—are told and retold by each generation until they pass from history into legend. Of the others, the ones whose names and deeds have been forgotten or, in some cases, banished from living memory, only StarClan knows.

THUNDERSTAR

Large orange tom the color of autumn leaves,
   with amber eyes and big white paws.
Strong, courageous, and determined.
Founder of ThunderClan—worked with Wind,
   Shadow, and River to develop the warrior
   code. According to legend it was Thunderstar
   who insisted on its more compassionate elements.
Deputies: Lightningtail, Owleyes (later Owlstar)
Apprentices: Unknown

OWLSTAR

Dark gray cat with large, unblinking amber eyes.
ThunderClan's second leader was a legendary hunter, who
   learned the ways of the tawny owl to stalk prey by night in
   silence.

Deputies: Unknown

Apprentices: Unknown

SUNSTAR

Tom with yellow tabby stripes, green eyes, and long fur.

Fair minded, even tempered, wise.

Held his Clan together through dangerous leaf-bare.

Fought to keep Sunningrocks away from RiverClan.

Deputies: Tawnyspots, Bluefur (later Bluestar)

Apprentice: Lionpaw (Lionheart)

BLUESTAR

Blue-gray she-cat with piercing blue eyes and silver hairs
tipping muzzle and tail.

Wise, kind, beloved, and strong.

Brought a kittypet named Rusty to join ThunderClan. Rusty
(renamed Firepaw, and later Fireheart) grew to become one
of the most essential, valued, and respected cats in all the
forest.

Deputies: Redtail, Lionheart, Tigerclaw, Fireheart (later Firestar)

Apprentices: Frostpaw (Frostfur), Runningpaw (Runningwind),
Firepaw (Fireheart)

FIRESTAR

Tom with bright green eyes and flame-colored pelt.

Brave, intelligent, loyal—a natural leader.

Has an unusually strong connection with StarClan, and is the
subject of StarClan's prophecy, "Fire alone can save our
Clan" (see *Prophecies and Omens*).

Brought WindClan back from exile after they were driven out
by ShadowClan.

Uncovered Tigerclaw's treachery in time to stop him killing
Bluestar.

Saved Clan from terrible fire in camp.

Discovered Tigerstar's scheme to unleash a pack of dogs to the
camp, and organized plan to save Clan.

Led the Clans of the forest against BloodClan.

Kept Clan together through the Twoleg destruction and brought
them safely to new lake home.

Deputies: Whitestorm, Graystripe, Brambleclaw

Apprentices: Cinderpaw (Cinderpelt), Cloudpaw (Cloudtail),
Bramblepaw (Brambleclaw)

SIGNIFICANT MEDICINE CATS

CLOUDSPOTS

Long-furred black tom with white ears, white chest, and two
white paws.

Inquiring, curious, and thoughtful, though sometimes appeared
shy and reserved.

Very interested in the theory of medicine—not quite so keen on
dealing with sickly kits.

Discovered the difference between greencough and
whitecough, and identified catnip as a possible cure. (See
*Beyond the Territories, How the Moonstone Was
Discovered.*)

FEATHERWHISKER

Pale, silvery gray tom with bright amber
    eyes, unusually long feathery whiskers,
    and a sweeping plume of a tail.

Sunstar's medicine cat and also his brother.

Gentle, sweet-natured, and kind mentor—
    passed on his compassion and deep
    connection with StarClan to his
    apprentice, Spottedleaf.

Worked tirelessly to save Clanmates during greencough
    epidemic, which ultimately killed him.

SPOTTEDLEAF

Beautiful dark tortoiseshell she-cat with amber eyes, white
    paws, black-tipped tail, and distinctive dappled coat.

Skilled interpreter of StarClan's mysterious messages.

Received StarClan prophecy that led Bluestar to bring Firepaw
    into Clan.

Walks dreams of ThunderClan cats, especially Firestar's.

YELLOWFANG

Ornery gray she-cat with bright orange
    eyes and broad, flattened face.

Gifted healer—could be bad-tempered
    and difficult.

Helped rescue ThunderClan kits from
    ShadowClan.

Became ThunderClan's medicine cat after Spottedleaf was killed.

Died as lived—fighting to save Clan.

CINDERPELT

Fluffy gray she-cat with enormous blue eyes.

Bright and energetic with boundless enthusiasm.

Quick learner—could have been agile warrior, were it not for injury.

Rescued two ShadowClan cats and nursed them back to health against orders.

Nursed Bluestar back to health when she contracted greencough.

Saved Brightpaw's life after the apprentice was mauled by the pack of dogs.

Died fighting to save Sorreltail.

LEAFPOOL

Small, light brown tabby with amber eyes, white paws, and white chest.

Quiet and soft-spoken—the opposite of her sister Squirrelflight!

Through their deep connection, she and her sister are able to share each other's feelings and dreams.

Found Moonpool—the place in Clans' new lake home where they can communicate with StarClan.

Saved RiverClan from deadly Twoleg poison by helping Hawkfrost, and helped Mothwing cure the cats.

Nursed Clan back to health after badger attack.

According to StarClan, Leafpool faces a destiny unlike any medicine cat before her.

WINDCLAN

TALLSTAR ON WINDCLAN

Welcome. I am Tallstar, and this is WindClan—
a Clan that has known great suffering, but always survives.
We are the fleet-footed warriors of the moor, the fastest Clan in the
forest. We have struggled through terrible hardship, but we never give up.
I know the other Clans sometimes see us as weak . . . but the truth is,
they could not last a moon in the broad, open spaces we live in,
chasing rabbits for our prey. We are the closest Clan to StarClan,
spiritually and physically, and we always know our warrior ancestors are
watching over us. That is what makes us strong. No matter what trials
we must endure, WindClan will last forever.

Clan character: Fiercely loyal, tough, fast-running, and easily offended cats. They are nervous and quick to flee, due
to the lack of cover on the open moor. They take pride
in being the closest Clan to the Moonstone. (See
Beyond the Territories, How the Moonstone Was Discovered.)
Of all the Clans, they have the deepest knowledge of
Twolegs from seeing them on the nearby farms.

Prey: Mainly rabbits.

Hunting skills: Fast, lean, and swift. Their short, smooth
pelts of browns and grays blend in with the rocks and
grasses.

WINDCLAN FOREST TERRITORY

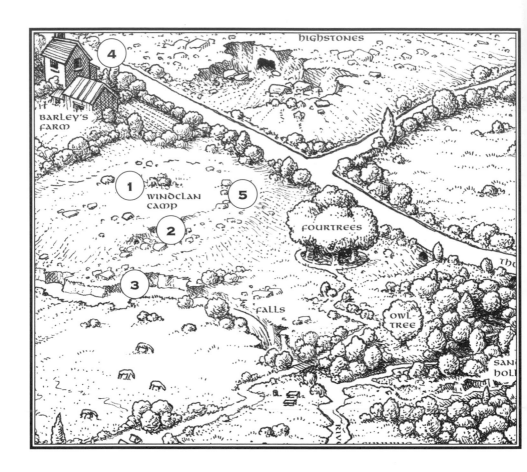

(1) WindClan camp: Tucked into a natural dip in the sandy moor, this camp is sheltered from the wind but has proved vulnerable to attack.

(2) Abandoned badger set: WindClan apprentices used to come here to learn the scent of badger. Now a great spot for hunting rabbits!

(3) The gorge: WindClan elders boast that they leaped all the way across in their youth, but apprentices are strictly forbidden to go too close.

(4) Twoleg farm: Cows, sheep, dogs, Twolegs, and two loner cats named Barley and Ravenpaw (see *Cats Outside the Clans, Rogues and Loners*) live here. WindClan sheltered in the barn on their way home from exile.

(5) Outlook Rock: This large, flat, gray stone slopes steeply above the level moors. From here, you can spot movement far across the grassland, especially a slow-moving or brightly colored cat from another Clan. WindClan apprentices are assigned to Outlook Rock to test their alertness and guard-duty skills.

WINDCLAN FOREST CAMP

Welcome to our camp! I'm Onewhisker, a warrior in WindClan, the greatest Clan in the forest.

You couldn't see our camp as you came this way, could you? That's because it's hidden in the only sheltered spot on the moor. It's a sandy hollow in the ground, surrounded by a tangle of gorse. The elders say that our first leader, Windstar, reached down from StarClan and scooped out a pawful of sand to make a hollow for us to live in.

Press through the prickly branches here and you'll be able to see the center of the camp. Breathe deeply. Don't you love the fresh air? It's so full of life and energy. I don't know how those other Clan cats live where they do. If I couldn't see the sky all day and all night, I'd go mad!

That's why the warriors sleep out here, under the stars, where our warrior ancestors can see us. It gives us a special connection to StarClan. We've had to deal with a lot of trouble and danger, but when I see them up there before I close my eyes, I know they're watching out for us.

Elders and kits can't sleep out in the open, though, so we've built dens for them along the edge of the gorse wall. And the leader has a den back behind the Tallrock, too, but he doesn't usually sleep there. Tallstar likes to sleep out in the open with us. What's the Tallrock? Oh, it's that large boulder over there from where Tallstar makes announcements and conducts ceremonies.

Hear that? It's an apprentice calling from Outlook Rock. That means there are trespassers in our territory! I'd better go chase them out.

Thanks for visiting!

RAID ON THE CAMP!

It was the darkest of nights. Heavy clouds flitted in front of a claw moon, blackening the sky. There were no StarClan ancestors watching over the WindClan camp that night.

At the camp entrance were two young warriors, Thrushwing and Stoneclaw. They had received their warrior names that night and were proudly standing guard.

Stoneclaw stood up, his ears pricked. What was that? A rustle in the gorse. A whisper of paws in the grass. A gleam of eyes in the darkness. What was that beyond the bushes? Should he sound the alarm?

Too late! A shadow appeared before him, and sharp claws slashed his throat. Thrushwing turned to see her brother lying on the ground, the life bleeding out of him. She shrieked a warning to the Clan, but the air was knocked out of her lungs by the weight of a large cat, and her voice died. Pinned to the ground, she felt the large cat's teeth stab at her neck as enemy cats poured past her into the clearing, moving swiftly, melting into the shadows.

Onewhisker was woken by Thrushwing's call. Beside him, Tornear and Deadfoot scrambled to their paws, and all three rushed into battle, sounding the WindClan warrior yowl.

"ShadowClan!" hissed Mudclaw from Tallrock. "I can smell their stink!" He launched himself off the boulder into the thick of the fighting, barreling into a hefty white tom.

"You're in no condition to fight!" Ashfoot growled at Morningflower, shoving the pregnant queen back into the nursery.

"But I want to fight!"

"Stay here and protect my son. I will fight."

Morningflower curled around the trembling gray shape of Eaglekit and licked the top of his head as comfortingly as she could. Ashfoot's enraged howls came from outside the tangle of branches.

Another WindClan warrior howled in fear, his belly sliced

open by a ShadowClan claw. Thrushwing had rejoined the battle and, in spite of an injured leg, fought like TigerClan to avenge the death of her brother. The bodies of two elders slumped next to a fallen apprentice. Deadfoot pounded over to Tallstar, his lame paw sending stabs of pain through him.

"They're going to kill us all!" he yowled. "We have to escape!"

"And abandon our camp?" Mudclaw hissed. "I'd rather die fighting than let these crow-food-eaters drive us out."

"Deadfoot's right," Tallstar meowed, his tail lashing furiously. "We've lost too many already. If we lose any more, there will be no more WindClan."

"Let's go, now," Deadfoot panted.

Tallstar ordered Onewhisker to fetch Morningflower and Eaglekit from the nursery. Then, the WindClan warriors and apprentices circled the queen and the two surviving elders and fought their way to the edge of the clearing. Morningflower was first to break through the gorse wall and run into the darkness, Ashfoot's kit bumping against her legs in terror. Thrushwing was next, supported by Onewhisker. One by one, the rest of WindClan followed, tearing through the gorse, their blood spattering the ground, until only Tallstar remained.

"This isn't the last of WindClan, Brokenstar," spat Tallstar.

"Wherever you run, I will find you," the enormous ShadowClan tabby hissed back at him.

And with that, Tallstar disappeared into the bushes, and WindClan left their home and fled into the night.

WINDCLAN LAKE
TERRITORY

(1) **Moonpool stream:** This tumbling stream leads along the edge of the WindClan border and up into the hills to the Moonpool (see *Beyond the Territories, the Moonpool*).

(2) **WindClan camp:** A shallow scoop in the ground, open to the sky. Unlike other cats, WindClan warriors prefer to sleep out in the open; in really bad weather, they retreat into underground burrows left by foxes and badgers.

(3) **Horseplace:** Hear that thundering? It's the pounding of horses' hooves! Stay on this side of the fence!

WINDCLAN LAKE CAMP

Can't you keep up? It must be true what they say about WindClan cats being faster than other cats! Come on, hurry!

Now, rest here and look down. See where my tail is pointing? That's our camp. It doesn't look protected, does it? You don't see any trees or rocks around it. But don't get any ideas! See how many heads are lifted down there? Half the warriors in our camp are watching you, sharpening their claws. No cat comes over these hills without being seen!

You might as well know that I'm Crowfeather and I brought WindClan to this place.

Let's go. Quickly! Follow me down—if you can keep up!

Now you are inside. Keep quiet and look only where I tell you.

This giant boulder is Tallrock, where Onestar makes his speeches. Yes, I know there are plenty of other boulders, but this is the biggest. Stop asking mouse-brained questions! Stop asking *any* questions!

This gorse bush against the boulder is the nursery. Move along—you'll scare the kits! Now, see this boulder? See the large crack in it? Smells like mouse bile, doesn't it? Our medicine cat, Barkface, is treating a tick problem in the camp. WindClan cats must have picked them up on the journey—all that hanging around among trees and swamps. *Blech!* Anyway, Barkface keeps his supplies in here. Any sick cat can sleep there too. If you ask me, fresh air is the best medicine. But what do I know?

See the tunnel under this gorse bush in the corner? It leads to an old badger set. You wouldn't catch me sleeping inside. It still stinks of badger. I sleep under the sky, near my warrior ancestors. Don't stick your nose in there! Rushtail might claw it off. It's the elders' den now.

So, that's the camp. You can tell Onestar I did as he asked. Now leave! Head straight up the hill and keep going until you see a bunch of large galumphing creatures with hooves. Horses, they're called. Past there is RiverClan territory—maybe they'll share their secrets with you next.

And remember . . . I'll be watching you go!

SIGNIFICANT LEADERS

WINDSTAR

Wiry brown she-cat with yellow eyes.

Proud, wily, stubborn, and fastest cat in the forest.

Founder of WindClan—worked with Thunder,
Shadow, and River to develop warrior
code.

Many of her descendants run with Clan
today, including current deputy,
Ashfoot, and Ashfoot's son
Crowfeather.

Deputies: Gorsefur (later Gorsestar)
Apprentices: Unknown

GORSESTAR

Thin gray tabby cat.

Remembered for his bravery and devotion to Windstar, his mate.

Deputies: Unknown
Apprentices: Unknown

TALLSTAR

Black-and-white tom with long tail and amber eyes.

One of the wisest and longest-lived WindClan leaders.

Unusually close to
    ThunderClan and
    particularly their
    leader Firestar.
Watched over Clan as
    they were forced
    out of home by
    ShadowClan.

One of first cats to argue for leaving the forest, according to the
    prophecy. (See *Prophecies and Omens.*) Frail and on last
    life, he led Clan to new home.
On his deathbed, Tallstar changed his deputy from Mudclaw to
    Onewhisker—a wise choice in the long run.
Deputies: Deadfoot, Mudclaw, Onewhisker (later Onestar)
Apprentice: Morningpaw (Morningflower)

ONESTAR

Small, mottled-brown tabby tom.
Loyal, devoted, strong, and compassionate.
Guided Clan through time of terrible tension after Tallstar made
    him leader in Mudclaw's place.
Survived rebellion against him.
First leader to receive nine lives at the Moonpool.
Took warriors to save ThunderClan when the badgers attacked.
Deputy: Ashfoot
Apprentices: Whitepaw (Whitetail), Gorsepaw

SIGNIFICANT MEDICINE CATS

MOTHFLIGHT

Soft white fur and stormy green eyes.

First WindClan medicine cat.

Loyal and true to her Clan, her restlessness, curiosity, and
dreaminess were at first deemed unwarriorlike.

These qualities gave her a new destiny, leading her to the
Moonstone.

THRUSHPELT

Stone-gray she-cat with flecks of darker brown fur.

Warrior for several moons before becoming WindClan
medicine cat.

Interpreted signs with immense confidence.

Expert herb finder.

Temperamental and quick to fight.

Took care of Clan through a sick-rabbit epidemic.

BARKFACE

Brown tom with stumpy tail.

Reliable, practical, and efficient.

Long, dependable service.

Received prophecy foretelling death at Gorge after WindClan
returned home. (See *Prophecies and Omens*.)

RIVERCLAN

Leopardstar on RiverClan

*There is a Clan unlike any other—a Clan
with all the strength, brilliance, and beauty of water.
Welcome to RiverClan. I am Leopardstar, the leader here.
Can you hear the river? In its flowing current you can
see what makes us the greatest Clan in the forest. Nothing can
stand against the force of water, just as nothing can defeat
RiverClan warriors when we rise up together. But when trouble
comes, RiverClan knows how to weave through the dangers,
adapting to the changed world, just as the river flows
around rocks and over waterfalls. We are grace.
We are power. We are RiverClan.*

Clan character: Contented, sleek, well fed. Long fur and glossy coats. They love beautiful things and often collect rocks, shells, and feathers for their dens. They do not fear water.

Prey: Mainly fish but also water voles, shrews, and mice.

Hunting skills: Strong swimmers, moving silent and scentless through water. They scoop fish out of the water from the bank—a skill most cats in the other Clans cannot master.

RIVERCLAN FOREST TERRITORY

(1) RiverClan camp: This well-drained island is circled by gently rustling reeds instead of thorns, but the other Clans' hatred of water means that it has never been attacked.

(2) The gorge: See *WindClan Forest Territory*.

(3) The river: It is a source of prey and protection to RiverClan, yet it is as changeable as the moon. Sometimes it is quiet, gentle, and murmuring, but sometimes it froths and roars like a Twoleg monster.

(4) Twoleg bridge: A safe way to cross the river and get to Fourtrees when the water is high.

RIVERCLAN FOREST CAMP

hi, I'm Feathertail. You'll have to get your paws wet if you want to see our camp. It's on an island! Don't be afraid of crossing; just listen to the murmur of the river—it's very soothing.

Under these long, trailing branches, that's right. They are willow trees. You should see them in leaf-bare after a frost. They sparkle like frozen raindrops!

All right, shake your paws, duck your head, and follow me through the reeds. The whole camp is surrounded by reeds, murmuring in the breeze. I love the sound they make, under the burble of the water. Look! It's our camp!

Here, in this central clearing, we lie in the sun and share tongues. In the mornings, I lie here and dry my fur after an early patrol. It's my favorite spot in the whole camp.

Here's the warriors' den, in this tangle of reeds. It's next to the nursery to protect the kits. Poke your head inside—it's all right; all the warriors are on patrol.

Look up at the roof of the den. See how we've woven feathers into the branches? And along the edges are sparkling rocks and shells from the river. They make the den shimmer, don't they? I love to lie in here, watching the lights and colors. It's just as beautiful in the nursery.

See how close the river comes to the nursery? Here, it's shallow and safe, but once before I was born, the river rose up suddenly and swept away the floor of the nursery and two kits—my mentor's kits. Now the walls are stronger. We like to have the kits living near water. They inherit our love of it and learn to swim quickly. Oh, look, they are practicing now!

You are doing wonderfully, kittens! Soon you'll be swimming faster than I can!

Across the clearing are the other dens, including Mudfur's—he's our medicine cat. Peek inside. You'll see that he makes small caves in the earth for the herbs. Now the kits can't scatter them when they run through his den chasing frogs.

On the other side of the island, a couple of rocks stick out of the river when the water isn't too high. They soak up the warmth of the sun. My favorite days begin with hunting with my brother, Stormfur, and end in the sun on those rocks. But you have to be fast. There is space for only a couple of cats, and if senior warriors or elders want them, you're out of luck. Our whole Clan could fit on Sunningrocks, where we used to bask. There was even room left for chasing prey and play-fighting. But I won't get into that now!

Uh-oh, it looks like rain. I'm going to curl up in the warriors' den and listen to the raindrops on the roof.

You should probably go too. But thank you for visiting!

FLOOD!

It was the coldest leaf-bare many cats could remember. The river turned to ice, trapping frosted reeds and cutting off RiverClan warriors from the fish. Prey on land was scarce.

With spring came the relentless *drip-drip* of melting ice. Cats grumbled about the soggy ground and the puddles in camp. But the worst was yet to come.

A young warrior, Silverstream, was on night watch. She listened to the roar of the river. It had been louder than usual for two days. The sun would be rising soon, and then she could nap. She stood up and stretched, padding off to patrol the boundary.

Sploosh! Silverstream jumped back. In the dark, she thought she had accidentally wandered off the island. No . . . the river must have risen. She padded over to her father's den.

"Crookedstar," she whispered. "There's something you should see."

The RiverClan leader followed his daughter to the camp entrance. The stream that separated them from the mainland had become a ribbon of dark, frothing water.

"The water is already moving fast," Silverstream meowed. "Should we evacuate the island?"

"It may go down again," Crookedstar meowed gruffly.

As the day went on, the water kept on rising, swirling through the reeds surrounding the camp. Mudfur moved his medicine cat supplies to a high rock, and the other cats watched the river nervously.

Leopardfur called Stonefur and Blackclaw to join her on patrol. "We'll see how far the floodwater reaches." The three warriors left the camp.

A yowl came from the end of the island.

Silverpaw and Shadepaw were scrabbling at the earth to try to block off a stream of water that had broken through the reeds. Loudbelly and Mistyfoot ran to help them.

"It's too strong!" Shadepaw yowled as the water burst into the camp.

Mistyfoot raced back toward the nursery. "Silverstream!" she yowled. "Help me!"

They scrambled inside to see brown water bubbling through the reeds and, in a corner, two kits mewled piteously, clawing at each other's fur. "My kits," Mistyfoot wailed, searching for the other two.

"They're gone!" Silverstream meowed above the sound of the rushing water. "But these two still need you!" She seized one kit in her jaws and backed out of the nursery.

Mistyfoot nudged the other kit. He opened his mouth and gave a small wail. She licked him, then picked him up and followed Silverstream to the river crossing.

The river gives us life, she thought, looking back at the flooded camp. *But now it's destroying us.* She placed a paw into the fast-moving water. *Oh, StarClan, how could you let this happen?*

Mudfur and Loudbelly stood downstream of the long line of cats, ready to catch them if they slipped or fell. No cat dared swim. The moment they lifted a paw off the pebble bed of the stream, the current tugged it away. Dark water swirled above their stomachs.

Crookedstar was last to cross. *We're no more powerful against this river than any other Clan,* he thought. *Everything that makes us RiverClan has been taken away from us.*

Mistyfoot and Silverstream scrambled out, the kits dangling from their jaws. The apprentices helped the elders ashore.

"Where do we go now?" Silverpaw meowed.

Crookedstar shook his fur. "The river is our home," he meowed. "StarClan will look after us." He nodded up the hill. "For now, we will rest in those bushes until Leopardfur's patrol returns."

Not long after they had settled in the shelter of the bushes, a yowl sounded from outside. Silverstream scented the air. ThunderClan! Graystripe!

She scrambled to her feet and pressed through the bushes to see the solid gray shape of the cat she loved best. Graystripe was sitting next to Fireheart. His eyes lit up when he saw her, and his tail flicked. Then she noticed the dripping bundles at the paws of Stonefur and Blackclaw.

Silverstream dashed to get Mistyfoot. "It's Fireheart and Graystripe," she panted. "They have your kits."

Silverstream had to compose herself before returning to Graystripe. She was so proud of him, and she was sure the other cats would sense it. She had to look as if he meant no more to her than any other cat.

Crookedstar listened to the story of the kits' rescue. *Is this how StarClan chooses to help us? By using enemy cats?* His throat was tight with injured pride that ThunderClan warriors could see the desperation of his Clan. But he knew that he could not refuse their help. It was a sign from StarClan. He would do whatever it took to save his Clan, and the river would be their home again soon.

RIVERCLAN LAKE TERRITORY

(1) **RiverClan camp:** Safely tucked away on a triangle of land between two streams, this camp is well sheltered from weather and enemy attack, with easy access to a constant source of prey.

(2) **Greenleaf Twolegplace:** A bees' nest of Twoleg activity during greenleaf! Twoleg kits jump into the lake with loud splashes and shrieks. Some of them can swim like RiverClan cats but more noisily.

(3) **Halfbridge:** A most peculiar bridge that ends halfway out in the water. It doesn't seem to go anywhere! Twolegs tie their "boats" to it.

RIVERCLAN LAKE CAMP

I know I'm biased—but RiverClan found the best lake home. Have you seen our camp? I'm Mistyfoot, by the way, the RiverClan deputy.

Before we go in, just look around you. The trees are lush, and the stream is full of fish. Back there is the lake. It's harder to catch fish in the lake than it was in the river, but we're learning. The biggest problem is the Twolegs. They love this place in greenleaf!

See where the smaller stream joins the main one? On the triangle of land between the streams is our camp. Can you swim across the stream like a RiverClan cat? Or will you splash through the shallows? You can also jump across on these pebble islands. Watch your step! Some of them are slippery!

Well done. You've made it. Now, look at all the vegetation! You can barely hear the noise of the Twolegs on the lake. See those

brambles? That is the nursery. Quite often there is a patch of sun-shine outside the entrance. In those thickets are the dens of the elders and Leopardstar.

Smell that? Sort of sharp and sweet at the same time? That's how you know we're near the medicine cat's den. Come around this thornbush—watch out for the prickles. See how it overhangs the stream? The earth below was washed away, leaving a pool in the roots and a hole in the bank where Mothwing keeps her supplies. She sleeps on that mossy nest. Oh, hello, Willowpaw!

Organizing berries, I see. Is Mothwing with Dawnflower? She was complaining of bellyache this morning. We'll just poke our heads in, take a sniff, and then leave you in peace.

One day this place will be as beautiful as our old camp. We haven't found as many shells in the water, but the Twolegs leave a lot of shiny things behind that our kits like to play with. We check everything carefully before we bring it into the camp, though. So many Twoleg things are bad for us!

Well, that's our camp. Watch your paws crossing the stream, and keep an eye out for Twolegs!

LEOPARDSTAR SPEAKS:
A Deadly Alliance

How dare you judge me? Have you been leader of a Clan? Have you had the fate of so many cats in your paws? Have you faced fire, flood, poison, starvation, predators, and Twolegs, all within a few short seasons? Kits and elders were dying under my watch. And I was supposed to sit back and let it all happen?

I am a great leader. I make tough decisions and stick to them. I discipline bad behavior with fair, strict punishment. My warriors respect me and would follow me to the end of the river if I told them to.

And I recognize strength when I see it. Tell me this—why is it all right for Crookedstar to accept help from those bleeding-heart ThunderClan warriors, but wrong for RiverClan to ally itself with Tigerstar? He has a plan for the forest—a vision for all the Clans! If you met him, you'd understand. He knows how we have suffered and how to save us. WindClan and ThunderClan will join us soon, I am sure.

As one Clan, we will rule the forest. No cat will go hungry. There will always be prey somewhere—in the river, in the woods, or on the moors—and all cats will benefit.

Why waste our energy fighting one another when our common enemies are dogs, badgers, and Twolegs? With the combined strength of all our warriors, perhaps we could fight back against the Twoleg monsters! Think of what we could accomplish! Think of how powerful we would be!

Tigerstar believes in TigerClan so strongly. I can see the future spreading out before us as he talks. If I join him now, he and I will be joint leaders. Tallstar and Firestar will have to follow us. I know that Tigerstar is in charge now, but this was his idea. Once everything is settled, he will listen to me.

And if TigerClan is inevitable, as I believe it is, I would rather be the second-strongest cat in the whole forest than cast out of the Clan to wander alone. Tigerstar has been there. He knows what it is to be weak and alone. He told me about it, and I never want to be that cat.

The only thing that makes me nervous is the way he keeps talking about half-Clan cats. I had no idea that Stonefur was half ThunderClan when I made him my deputy. Neither did he, in fact. But now we know he is, he and his sister, Mistyfoot. And half-Clan cats cannot be trusted, Tigerstar says.

He has a point—remember what happened with Graystripe? I always suspected he was spying on us, waiting for a chance to tell ThunderClan our secrets. He betrayed us in the end. Divided loyalties are not what TigerClan needs if we want to survive all the troubles facing us.

I don't know what Tigerstar plans to do with our half-Clan cats, but I know something must be done. For now, I've allowed him to leave a few ShadowClan warriors in our camp to protect us. They're not like RiverClan cats. They're building a hill of prey bones down by the riverbank. It gives me nightmares. . . .

SIGNIFICANT LEADERS

RIVERSTAR

Silvery gray, long-furred tom with green eyes.

Generous and warm-hearted with his own
Clan—uninterested in the troubles of other
Clans. (Would skip Gatherings if he could!)

Founder of RiverClan—worked with Thunder,
Shadow, and Wind to develop warrior code.

Thought to have suggested mentoring program of training
apprentices.

Deputies: Unknown
Apprentices: Unknown

CROOKEDSTAR

Huge light-colored tabby tom with green
eyes and twisted jaw.

Determined, strong, and willing to bend the
rules for safety of Clan.

Guided Clan through terrible leaf-bare and flood.

Accepted help from ThunderClan warriors to save Clan from
starving.

Offered shelter to ThunderClan when fire drove them from their
home.

Deputy: Leopardfur (later Leopardstar)
Apprentices: Graypaw (Graypool), Stonepaw (Stonefur)

LEOPARDSTAR

Spotted golden tabby she-cat.

Proud, hostile, and fierce. Single-minded about what is best for RiverClan. Showed bad judgment in turning over control of RiverClan to Tigerstar.

As deputy, she helped ThunderClan when they fled the fire in their camp.

Also led her Clan to their new lake home, where she quickly established a strong base.

Deputies: Stonefur, Mistyfoot, Hawkfrost (temporarily)

Apprentices: Whitepaw (Whiteclaw), Hawkpaw (Hawkfrost)

SIGNIFICANT MEDICINE CATS

DAPPLEPELT

Delicate tortoiseshell she-cat.

Brave, reckless, quick to act.

Saw being a medicine cat as a different type of warrior, fighting the invisible enemies of sickness and injury on behalf of her Clanmates.

Saved an entire litter of kits after the nursery was washed away by a flood. (See *Beyond the Territories, How the Moonstone Was Discovered.*)

BRAMBLEBERRY

Pretty white she-cat with black-spotted fur, blue eyes, and a strikingly pink nose.

Charming, quick-thinking, and good at getting her own way—
Crookedstar would do anything she asked.

Cautious about interpreting StarClan's omens.

Came up with a clever way to hide medicinal herbs in fresh-kill
so sick kits would eat them.

MUDFUR

Long-haired, light brown tom.

Patient, intelligent, and straightforward.

Interpreted moth's wing sign to choose his new apprentice,
despite her non-Clan origins.

MOTHWING

Beautiful dappled-golden she-cat with large amber eyes in a
triangular face, and a long pelt rippling with dark tabby
stripes.

The daughter of a rogue cat, Sasha, and the former leader of
ShadowClan, Tigerstar, Mothwing struggles for acceptance by
her Clan.

Believes StarClan does not exist.

With Leafpool's help, healed her Clan when kits brought traces of
Twoleg poison back to camp.

SHADOWCLAN

BLACKSTAR ON SHADOWCLAN

Greetings. I am Blackstar. You must be brave indeed,
to approach the territory of ShadowClan. Few are welcome here,
in our world of secrets and darkness. We are a Clan of
cunning and cleverness, a Clan well suited to the shadows and
the cold north wind. No other Clan can walk the paths of night like
we do. Other Clans may be faster or stronger, but we are the
most dangerous warriors: fierce, proud, and independent. We are
ruthlessly willing to do what it takes to protect our great Clan.
There won't be any softhearted alliances here! ShadowClan
will always be the dark heart of the forest.

Clan character: Battle-hungry, aggressive, ambitious, and greedy for territory. It is said that the cold wind that blows across the ShadowClan territory chills their hearts and makes them suspicious and untrusting.

Prey: Frogs, lizards, and snakes that live in ShadowClan's boggy, peaty territory. A secret food source is the Twoleg garbage dump on the far boundary, although they have to be careful not to eat infected rats or crow-food.

Hunting skills: ShadowClan cats hunt by night better than other Clan cats and are skilled at skulking unseen through the undergrowth.

---

shadowclan forest territory

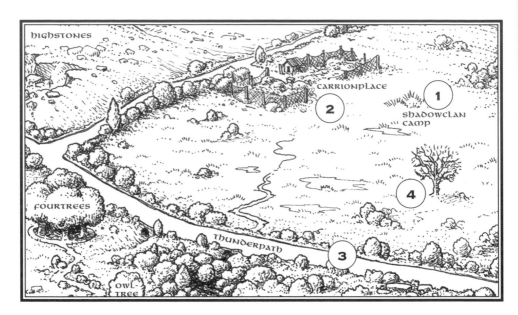

(1) ShadowClan camp: A dark, well-concealed hollow, the camp is
hidden deep in the shadows and is surrounded by brambles
as prickly and fierce as the hearts of ShadowClan warriors.

(2) Carrionplace: Yuck! Smell that? This is an evil place where rats
and disease lurk.

(3) Thunderpath tunnel: The ability of ShadowClan cats to move
freely across the most feared border of the Thunderpath has
enhanced their reputation for mysterious strength and
invincibility.

(4) Burnt Sycamore: An ancient tree destroyed by lightning
many moons ago. Apprentices are often trained
here to hunt at night and stalk noiselessly
through the undergrowth.

shadowclan forest camp

My name is Boulder. Ah, I can see you've realized it's not a warrior name. Well, I used to be a loner in Twolegplace, and proud of it. I caught prey for myself. I could look after myself. Then I met a cat from ShadowClan. He told me about the forest. He wanted me to give up my freedom and join his Clanmates! I nearly clawed off his fur. I didn't need a leader or a Clan.

But he kept talking, and some of the things he said made sense. Like, what was I going to do when I was old and couldn't catch my own prey? I'd never thought about that before.

I agreed to visit his camp. Follow me, and you'll see what I saw on that day I first came to the forest. I've never left since.

I love the forest on this side of the Thunderpath. The soft carpet of pine needles under my paws. The fresh and sharp smell of the pines. The boggy soil is full of amazing smells; can you sense prey darting around under the leaves?

Through these brambles, that's right. This tiny path—here, where my paws are—leads to a hollow. I know it's not exactly grassy around here, but the ground is muddy and cool. Good for keeping fresh-kill fresh. Our leader sleeps over there, beneath the roots of that big oak tree. The warriors' den is over there, underneath the bramble bush. I know it looks prickly on the outside, but inside it's lined with pine needles and moss. I can tell you, it's a lot more comfortable than any place I found to stretch my paws in Twolegplace.

The smooth boulder at the edge of the clearing is where the leader speaks to us. Do you see that other rock propped against it, creating a sheltered half cave underneath? That's where the medicine cat lives. There are holes dug in the ground to keep the leaves and berries fresh, and sick cats can rest in the ferns that grow on the other side of the boulders. I never had another cat care about my injuries when I lived in Twolegplace.

The nursery's over there, in that hollow shielded by a thornbush. You can smell the scent of milk from here—a new litter was born yesterday. I don't spend much time with the tiniest kits—always worried I'll step on them or something— but I like watching them grow into strong apprentices and loyal warriors.

Why do you keep staring at the fresh-kill pile? Oh, I see you've spotted a frog. I know they look pretty unappetizing—trust me, I was as reluctant as you to try them when I first came to the forest. But you should try them. Peel off the skin first—that's very chewy. Underneath, it tastes like if you mixed rabbits and fish together. Honestly! Well, okay, maybe leave it for one of the warriors. Look, I know the other Clans think ShadowClan cats are strange and dark-hearted, but we're loyal warriors, just like them. There's no need to fear us.

Not all of the time, anyway.

shadowclan lake
territory

(1) **ShadowClan camp:** Much closer to Twolegs than forest home,
  but the camp is still well hidden and should be difficult for
  enemies to attack.

(2) **Twoleg nest:** Home to two aggressive kittypets. Don't let them
  catch you out alone, or you're kittypet food!

(3) **Twoleg path:** Steer clear of these during greenleaf. Twolegs
  tramp up and down these paths all season long!

(4) **Greenleaf Twolegplace:** Another place haunted throughout
  greenleaf by Twolegs, who put up small dens and build
  terrifying little fires here. On the plus side, sometimes they
  leave behind food like we used to find at Carrionplace.

shadowclan lake camp

I never thought Blackstar would let you into the ShadowClan camp. He's a little prickly mostly. But we like having a cat in charge who says exactly what he thinks.

I'm Tawnypelt, and I found this place—you've heard about that?

I tell you, by the time we found the camp, I was getting worried. The territory looked right—pine trees everywhere, shadows, and darkness. But the tree branches were much higher than we were used to, and there wasn't much undergrowth.

It was getting dark when we came up this slope here. Did you see the pool down at the bottom? It's close to the camp so we can fetch water for the elders and kits without having to go all the way to the lake. Here, follow me up these boulders until we get to that top one—it's got the best view of the camp.

Great, isn't it? You can barely tell there are so many cats down there, hidden below the tangles of brambles. And look at all these low-hanging branches all around and above us. You won't catch us getting trampled by badgers like ThunderClan!

Not that we're cowards, mind you. Every ShadowClan cat, down to the tiniest kit, will fight to the death to defend our territory and our pride. We're the fiercest Clan in the forest, no matter what any other cat might say.

I wasn't born a ShadowClan cat—but I'm very glad I'm here now. I like being ferocious, and I like hunting in the dark. You won't find me lolling around in the sun like those RiverClan cats or crashing through the forest making as much noise as a ThunderClan cat.

But we can have fun too. Smokepaw and I like to climb trees near the lake and watch the Twolegs on the water. Their boats look like swan wings. The Twolegs make a lot of noise and splashing, and sometimes the boats tip over and they fall in! Then they get back up and fluff out their wings to try again. You've never seen anything so funny. I would never set paw on a boat—leave that to the RiverClan cats!

Anyway, slip on through these bramble bushes and you can see the camp. Like in the old camp, there is a clear progression of dens from one side to the other: nursery first, then the apprentices' den, then the warriors, the leader, and the elders at the end of the circle. That puts the kits and elders closest to the lowest-hanging branches and leaves the warriors facing the entrance, in case of trouble.

The medicine cat's den is in that far corner, beyond the leader's den. Littlecloud found a place where the branches aren't so bunched together—he needs to see the sky so he can read the signs from our warrior ancestors.

Blackstar makes his announcements from the branch that hangs over his den. You should see him swarm up that tree when he's angry!

So that's our camp. I'd let you poke your nose into the dens, but ShadowClan cats aren't friendly to strangers. Even though Blackstar said it would be okay, I think you should keep your stay as short as possible. And if I were you, I wouldn't linger on ShadowClan territory. Head this way, cross a stream, and you'll hit ThunderClan's part of the forest. You'll be perfectly safe there. They take in strays all the time, those softhearted geese.

Bye now!

SIGNIFICANT LEADERS

SHADOWSTAR

Black she-cat with green eyes and
thick fur.

A strategist, ferociously independent
(even untrusting of Clanmates),
bold in battle.

Founder of ShadowClan—worked with Thunder, Wind, and
River to develop warrior code (she spent the rest of her
life complaining about it).

First of founding leaders to die—losing ninth life in battle she
started with other Clans.

Deputies: Unknown

Apprentices: Unknown

RAGGEDSTAR

Large dark brown tabby. Fur ragged and patchy from fighting
as a kit.

Proud and cunning—failed to see his son Brokentail's
bloodthirsty nature until too late.

Defeated rats in violent battle near Carrionplace that kept
them from bothering ShadowClan for many moons.

Deputies: Foxheart, Cloudpelt, Brokentail (later Brokenstar)

Apprentices: Clawpaw (Clawface), Brokenpaw (Brokentail)

BROKENSTAR

Long-haired dark brown tabby with torn ears and a broad, flat face. Tail bent in middle like broken branch.

Cold, ambitious, heartless, murderous, and cruel.

Killed own father, Raggedstar.

Weakened Clan by focusing its energies on war, apprenticing kits too early, and forcing Clan to eat crow-food instead of prey.

Blinded and killed by own mother, Yellowfang.

Deputy: Blackfoot (later Blackstar)

Apprentices: Mosspaw, Volepaw (both died mysteriously before becoming warriors)

NIGHTSTAR

Elderly black tom.

Brave but frail.

Took over leadership when Brokenstar was driven into exile.

Struggled to rebuild broken Clan—StarClan did not grant him the nine lives of a leader.

Died from sickness from Carrionplace shortly after his deputy died, leaving Clan target for Tigerstar's ambitions.

Deputy: Cinderfur

Apprentice: Dawnpaw (Dawncloud)

TIGERSTAR

Large dark brown tabby tom with amber eyes and long front claws.

Ambitious, crafty, charismatic, and brilliant fighter.

Exiled by Bluestar after attempt on her life.

After period in exile, gained leadership of ShadowClan—
    rebuilding it with exceptional efficiency.

Allied ShadowClan with RiverClan to make TigerClan.

Brought BloodClan into forest at cost of many cats' lives.

Killed by Blood, the leader of BloodClan.

Deputy: Blackfoot (later Blackstar)

Apprentice: Ravenpaw (while in ThunderClan)

BLACKSTAR

Large white tom with huge jet-black paws.

Arrogant and defensive. Tigerclaw brought him back to
    ShadowClan from exile—he still feels a hint of gratitude
    and loyalty toward the dangerous tabby.

Led Clan away from Twoleg devastation in the forest to new
    lake home.

Deputy: Russetfur

Apprentice: Tallpaw (Tallpoppy)

SIGNIFICANT MEDICINE CATS

PEBBLEHEART

Dark gray tabby tom.

Selfless, caring, desperate to help his
    Clanmates with any problem.
    Weakened himself by working tirelessly.

Realized that rats at Carrionplace were a source of infection.
(Unfortunately he died from a rat-borne infection.) (See
*Beyond the Territories, How the Moonstone Was
Discovered.*)

YELLOWFANG

(See *ThunderClan Medicine Cats, Yellowfang.*)

RUNNINGNOSE

Small gray-and-white tom with perpetual sniffle.
Nervous and quiet. Lived long enough to retire and become an
elder.
Apprentice: Littlecloud

LITTLECLOUD

Undersize brown tabby tom with light blue eyes.
Compassionate and devoted to his calling.
Close friends with ThunderClan medicine cat Cinderpelt ever
since she saved his life.
As a warrior, sought help from ThunderClan during time of
terrible disease. Returned with remedy that saved
ShadowClan.

YELLOWFANG SPEAKS:
A Thankless Kit

As soon as I found out I was going to have kits, I knew it was a punishment from StarClan. Medicine cats are not supposed to fall in love. My relationship with Raggedstar was wrong in every way, and I knew it.

But I never expected all of ShadowClan would be punished for my mistakes.

I kept my secret well. No cat knew that their medicine cat was carrying kits, although of course I told Raggedstar. He was so pleased. . . . That should have frightened me even more. The arrogance of thinking we could do whatever we wanted, without consequences . . .

It was a hard birth, a horrible birth. That was an omen too. I snuck out of camp that morning, knowing my kits were coming. I found a hollow in a dead tree, filled with damp leaves. There was a smell of toadstools and something rotting, but I didn't have the strength to drag myself any farther. And I hoped the stench would hide my scent while I gave birth, alone in the woods. I didn't want any ShadowClan cats to find me, not even Raggedstar. I just wanted it to be over.

I felt like I was lying in that dead tree for days. Everything hurt—my whole body, down to the tips of my fur and the ends of my claws. As a medicine cat, I should have been able to take care of myself, but I was too weak to do anything, even eat the herbs I'd brought.

Finally there were three small bundles next to me on the pile of leaves. Two of them were squirming; one was completely still. I prodded it with my paw, but she had been born dead. Her eyes would never open.

I dragged the other two toward me. With all the strength I could manage, I began to lick them, trying to warm them and wake them up. One let out an angry wail the minute I touched him; the other only whimpered slightly and jerked her paws. I could see that the tom kit was a fighter right from the beginning. His lungs were so powerful, I was surprised it didn't bring the entire Clan running to find us. He battered his sister with his paws every time he moved, but she barely reacted.

I tried as long as I could, licking and licking her, but her breathing only got shallower and shallower, until finally it stopped altogether. Her tail twitched once and was still. I buried my nose in her fur, feeling grief crash down on me. It was a clear sign from StarClan. These kits should never have been born.

I turned my attention to my only surviving kit and saw the expression on his small, flat face. He was new to the world—couldn't yet see, could barely crawl to my belly to feed. And yet his face was already twisted with strong emotion. . . . Rage? Hatred? I'd never seen such a terrifying look on any cat, let alone a tiny newborn kit.

Fear flooded through me, making me cold. Maybe this kit wasn't meant to survive, either. A kit born with so much anger in him could mean only grave danger to the Clan, maybe to the whole forest.

But then he squirmed over to me and pressed his face into my fur. He was so small, so helpless. Perhaps I had misunderstood what I'd seen. He was only a little kit, after all—my kit, and the son of Raggedstar, the cat I loved. I couldn't keep him for myself, but I could watch him from across the clearing as he grew up. I could make sure he turned into a fine warrior. I licked the top of his head, and he let out a small purr. My heart seemed to expand to fill my whole chest.

I buried his sisters before we returned to camp, digging deep into the dirt so no cat would ever sniff them out. Then I slunk back through the undergrowth, my fur matted and stinking of toadstools, the kit dangling from my mouth. I stopped to clean myself in a pool near the camp entrance. By the time we entered the camp, no cat would be able to guess the ordeal I had been through.

Raggedstar spotted us the minute I pushed through the bramble tunnel. He barely even looked at me; his eyes were all for the kit, and they were full of hope and excitement. He came bounding across the clearing to follow me into the nursery.

Lizardstripe was there, of course, tending to her own two kits, born a few days earlier. Her pale brown tabby fur and white under-belly seemed to glow in the darkness of the nursery den. She looked at me with narrow, unfriendly eyes. I had never really liked or trusted Lizardstripe, but she was the only nursing queen at the moment. I had no choice.

I dropped the kit at her paws, and he let out another furious shriek.

"What," said Lizardstripe, "is *that*?"

"It's a kit," I said.

"It's *my* kit," Raggedstar said proudly, shouldering his way into the den.

"Oh, yes?" Lizardstripe said dryly. "What a miracle. If I'd known toms could have kits, I would have made Mudclaw have these brats of mine himself."

Raggedstar ignored her. The space seemed to get smaller with him in it, as if he drew all the light into himself. I wanted to press myself into his fur and tell him everything I'd been through and about the two tiny bodies out in the forest. But he still wasn't looking at me.

He crouched and sniffed at his son. The kit tried to lift his head and then swiped his paw through the air, connecting with Raggedstar's nose. Our leader jerked his head back in surprise.

"Look at that!" he cried delightedly. "He's a little warrior already!"

Lizardstripe's yellow gaze was making me uncomfortable. "His mother wishes to keep her identity secret," I said. "She cannot be a mother to this kit, and she hopes that you will take him in for her."

Lizardstripe lashed her tail. "What kind of mouse-brained nonsense is that?" she snapped. "Why should I have to put up with another mewling lump of fur? I didn't ask for these kits, either, but you don't see me dumping them on some other cat. It's not my job to take care of every unwanted kitten in the Clan."

Raggedstar snarled, and Lizardstripe shrank back in her nest. "He is *not* unwanted," Raggedstar spat. "He is my son, and I will always claim him as my own. You are being given a great honor, you unworthy cat. Who wouldn't want to be mother to the Clan leader's son—and perhaps the future leader of the Clan himself?"

Lizardstripe hissed softly. But she knew better than to argue with Raggedstar. And perhaps she saw the wisdom of his words. As the mother of Raggedstar's son—even if the Clan knew she wasn't his real mother—she would hold power in the Clan.

"All right, fine," she spat ungraciously. "Hand him over."

As I nestled my son into the curve of her belly, I felt a strong pang of uneasiness. What kind of life would he have, with an ambitious queen like Lizardstripe raising him? No cat would know I was his mother, not even the kit himself. I would never be able to sway him to be good, to follow the warrior code and believe in the wisdom of StarClan. I would just have to hope that he would turn out all right.

"His name is Brokenkit," I said, my voice faltering. Lizardstripe nodded, seeing the bend in his tail, like a broken branch. That's where every cat would think he'd gotten his name. But the truth is, I named him for the feeling in my chest as I left him there, as if my heart were breaking in two, as if my life had broken down the middle.

Most cats assumed that Raggedstar's deputy, Foxheart, was Brokenkit's mother. She was always a little secretive, and he let her get away with a lot. She never contradicted the rumors; it was to her advantage to let other cats think she was the secret mother of Raggedstar's kit. She died a few moons later, anyway, in a battle with rats near Carrionplace, shortly before Lizardstripe died of greencough. The next deputy, Cloudpelt, didn't last much longer than they did, and by then Brokentail was old enough for Raggedstar to make him deputy.

Raggedstar always thought his son would make a great leader. He was blind to all of Brokentail's faults—his cunning, his ruthlessness, his violent nature. Raggedstar didn't care for me anymore. His life was all about Brokentail from the moment he laid eyes on that kit.

My punishment stretched on as Brokentail clawed his way to power, and I realized what a monster I'd brought into the forest. But it was my mistake, and I had to live with it. And there was a part of me that still remembered him as a newborn kit—the tiny scrap of fur I nursed in the hollow of a dead tree.

When I had to kill him to protect my new adopted Clan, I knew I was finally at the end of my punishment. I had brought him into the world; I had to send him out, as painful as it was.

But by then I had found a truer son than Brokentail ever could have been. I only hope Fireheart will rise to be the great leader that Brokenstar never was and that, in some small way, I have helped to set him on that path.

Then, perhaps, StarClan will forgive me at last.

STARCLAN

Wait until it is dark and the night sky is full of stars. Can you hear them? Do they whisper to you of secret places and adventures? Follow the path of the moon through the forest. Feel the bracken crackle under your paws and the wind ruffle your fur. Mist curls around you and blurs the familiar shapes of the forest. Press through the ferns until you come out into a clearing.

Towering over you are four giant oaks, massive and dark, outlined by the moonlight. In the center of the clearing, on the Great Rock, I will be waiting for you.

I am Lionheart. I was a ThunderClan warrior. In a fierce battle, I died defending my Clan. Now I belong to StarClan, a Clan of the spirits of our warrior ancestors.

Yes, you are dreaming. We often walk in the dreams of those we watch. Don't be afraid. I know it looks like a land of mist and shadows, but I promise there is enough light to warm the darkest of hearts.

From here, we watch over the Clans we have left behind.

The saddest moments are when kits come to join us, whether through illness, predators, or unexpected disaster. But we love it when new kits are born, and my heart swells with pride every time a ThunderClan apprentice becomes a warrior.

Sometimes we can sense the destiny of these warriors. It is clearest with new leaders. When Firestar became leader of ThunderClan, I could see that he would lead the Clan through terrible times with courage and wisdom. When Tigerstar rose to power in ShadowClan, we all knew that darkness lay ahead.

Sadly, we cannot change what will happen to the cats we watch. I would have done anything to prevent the fire that swept through ThunderClan territory or to save my Clanmates from the dog pack. But the lives of warriors are filled with tragedy, and there's nothing we can do to stop it. All we can do is warn our descendants with signs and prophecies and hope that they listen.

The cats with the closest bond to StarClan usually become medicine cats. Spottedleaf had a particularly special connection to us; Firestar's daughter Leafpool does as well. Firestar himself often has prophetic dreams—he even had them when he was a kittypet. These cats meet us in their dreams. They can read the omens we paint in the sky or the leaves or the water. They know the meaning of a falling star or a strange cloud pattern. We need them to understand us, so they can keep our Clans safe.

There are sacred places too, which inhabit both the world of living cats and the world of dreams. Here leaders may come to receive visions and seek our guidance. We also grant them nine lives and their star name.

We most often speak to cats of our own Clans. Yet, sometimes, we reach out to cats of other Clans. I understand the other Clans better than I did when I was alive. I wish them well, even the cats I fought. We need all four Clans to survive.

Cats who have caused great pain in their lives wander a strange forest of darkness in death. We sense this distant place. Tigerstar, Brokenstar, Clawface, and Darkstripe are there, exiled from the Clan of their ancestors, of no comfort to one another.

There are other skies where other cats walk as well. The Tribe of Rushing Water have ancestors of their own, and while our questing cats were in the mountains, we could not see them clearly. They were in the territory of different spirits, where we couldn't go.

On the journey to the lake, we had trouble reaching our warriors. We had to travel ourselves, through unfamiliar sky paths, to find our new home. We could not have found it without them, and they could not have found it without us.

Are you wondering how we can be here, at Fourtrees, if the forest has been destroyed by Twolegs? Don't worry. Fourtrees will always be in our hearts. It is a part of StarClan too, wherever we are.

Now return to your den and your peaceful dreams. Thank you for visiting StarClan. Remember, keep your eyes and ears open, watch for anything unusual, and you too may see the signs we leave in the world around you.

SNOWFUR SPEAKS:
A Sad, Cold Death

My name is Snowfur, and I am now one of the warrior ancestors. I came to StarClan as a young warrior, killed by a Twoleg monster while I was chasing ShadowClan intruders out of our territory. I mourned along with my Clan, but not for my own life. I only wished I could have stayed until my son became a warrior. Of course, I watched his ceremony from the stars, a few moons later. Whitestorm was so excited, so brave, and I was so proud of him. I think he knew I was there with him during his vigil.

It was not long after that when we learned that my sister, Bluefur, was having kits. I wished we could just be happy for her, but she had broken the warrior code, and I knew it was going to bring her much sorrow. The father of the kits was not ThunderClan. He was the RiverClan deputy, Oakheart.

"A kit is coming to join us," Brambleberry, the former RiverClan medicine cat, meowed. "Half ThunderClan, half RiverClan."

"Half-Clan!" spat a ShadowClan warrior.

"It is an innocent kit," Brambleberry meowed with fierce anger in her voice.

The cats of StarClan were gathered at Fourtrees, which was blanketed by snow just like the whole forest in the world of our descendants. It was a bitter leaf-bare, and many cats were starving. More cats came to StarClan every day, and we were all feeling frustrated that there was nothing we could do to help.

"This kit did not have to die," hissed Moonflower. She was my and Bluefur's mother, but she did not approve of what my sister was doing. "It is Bluefur's fault for falling in love outside the Clan in the first place. And now she is dragging her three helpless kits out into the snow with her! Of course one of them is going to die. I'm amazed the other two will make it as far as RiverClan."

"But they will be safer there than they were in ThunderClan," meowed a RiverClan spirit. "RiverClan has more prey than any other Clan. If Oakheart will take them in, they have a better chance of survival than they did before."

"We don't know that," Moonflower meowed. "If she had kept them safely in our den, all three of them might have lived to be warriors."

"And what else lies along that path?" meowed Owlstar, one of the oldest ThunderClan spirits. "Study that future carefully, Moonflower."

"It is too dark to see it clearly," she protested.

"But we can guess," Owlstar murmured. "If Bluefur stays in the nursery with her kits, Thistleclaw will become deputy instead. He is an ambitious, violent cat, and we know it. He would lead his warriors to attack other Clans—the last thing this forest needs right now. Would you rather see more warriors coming to join us because of his bloody leadership?"

"So a kit's life is the price to be paid for the warriors whom Thistleclaw *might* lead into death," Moonflower growled. "I know that Bluefur believes Thistleclaw would be the wrong leader for ThunderClan. But how do we know that being deputy wouldn't make him a better cat?"

"We don't know," Brambleberry meowed. "And neither does Bluefur. She must make her choices based on what she thinks might happen. I don't agree with what she's doing . . . I would never endanger innocent kits . . . but I can see why she's doing it."

"It is for the good of the Clan," Owlstar meowed.

"But not for the good of the kit," Moonflower spat.

"We cannot change what will happen to Mosskit," Brambleberry meowed. "We can only make sure he is protected on his journey to StarClan."

"I will take care of him," I spoke up. The others all looked around at me. "I was a queen when I died," I pointed out. "My son, Whitepaw, had only recently left the nursery. I remember well how to care for kits . . . and I miss it. I would be a good mother to this kit."

Owlstar nodded. "I think Snowfur is right. She would be a good choice."

"I agree," Brambleberry meowed.

Moonflower nodded as well, her eyes soft and sad.

I slipped away from the group and followed the edge of the river down toward Sunningrocks. My paws skimmed the smooth pebbles like I was swimming over them. I could feel the cold blasts of wintry air in the forest world, although they could not pierce my thick white fur.

A few fox-lengths into the trees, I found Bluefur curled around three small gray shapes. She was lucky they all looked like her, I thought—if any had had Oakheart's coloring, some cat in ThunderClan might have suspected her secret by now. Two of the kits were squirming and protesting as Bluefur licked them. The third seemed to be sleeping in the snow. This was Mosskit.

Bluefur kept nudging him with her nose. Her eyes were pools of grief, and I could feel it with her. The snow buffeted her sides, where her ribs were showing through her thin gray fur, but she kept meowing: "Oh, Mosskit! What have I done? Mosskit, please wake up

Mosskit, don't leave. There's warmth and safety just on the other side of the river. Your father will look after you, I promise. Just a little bit farther, my tiny, brave son." She crouched closer to him, gathering him between her paws. "Mosskit, how could I do this to you?"

My heart ached for her, but it was too late. Mosskit had crossed over into my world. I ducked my head and whispered, "Mosskit, wake up."

The dark gray kit opened his eyes and looked at me. "Who are you?" he squeaked. "Why do you have stars in your fur?"

"Don't be scared," I murmured. "I'm Snowfur. I'm here to take care of you."

Mosskit shook himself and staggered toward me on tiny paws. His spirit nuzzled into my fur. Behind him, his body was still curled beside Bluefur, but Mosskit didn't notice.

"I'm cold," he protested. "I'm so cold. Cold all the way to the tip of my tail. My whiskers are frozen, look."

"I know," I meowed, licking the top of his head. "Come with me, and you will be warm."

Mosskit hesitated, looking up at me with wide green eyes. "What about my mother?"

"She'll be all right," I meowed. It was true. It would be hard for a long time, and she would never forget Mosskit, but she would push aside the memory and focus on her Clan. She would survive.

"But I want to be with her," Mosskit whimpered. "I want my mother and Mistykit and Stonekit."

"You will see them again," I promised. "You will watch over them from the stars until they come to join you."

He pressed his face into my fur and nodded. I looked back at my sister one more time, and then Mosskit and I walked away, following the moonlight back into the stars.

TERRITORIES

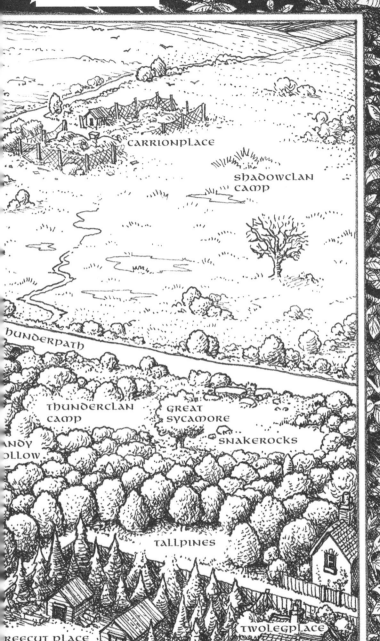

THE FOREST

CARRIONPLACE

SHADOWCLAN CAMP

THUNDERPATH

THUNDERCLAN CAMP

GREAT SYCAMORE

SNAKEROCKS

SANDY HOLLOW

TALLPINES

TREECUT PLACE

TWOLEGPLACE

THUNDERCLAN

RIVERCLAN

SHADOWCLAN

WINDCLAN

STARCLAN

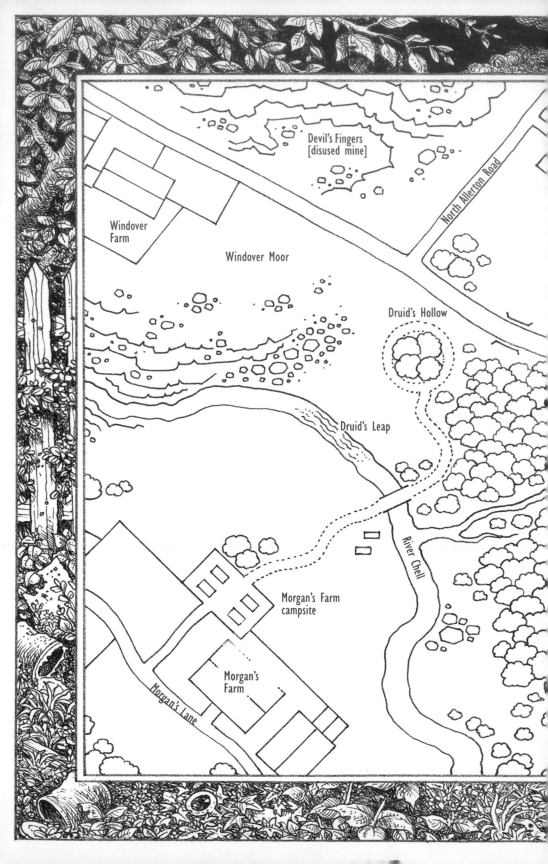

Devil's Fingers
[disused mine]

North Allerton Road

Windover
Farm

Windover Moor

Druid's Hollow

Druid's Leap

River Chell

Morgan's Farm
campsite

Morgan's
Farm

Morgan's Lane

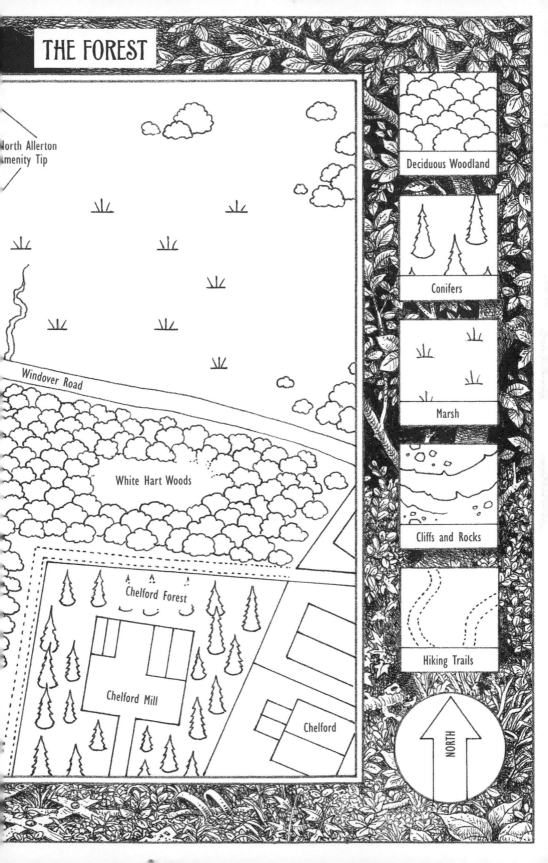

THE FOREST

North Allerton
Amenity Tip

Windover Road

White Hart Woods

Chelford Forest

Chelford Mill

Chelford

Deciduous Woodland

Conifers

Marsh

Cliffs and Rocks

Hiking Trails

NORTH

BEYOND THE TERRITORIES

FOURTREES

In a clearing at the center of the forest, where all four Clan territories converge, there is a space sacred to StarClan. Four great oaks stand at the corners of the clearing. At one end is a large boulder called the Great Rock, where the Clan leaders stand during Gatherings. Every month, at the full moon, cats from all four Clans gather here in peace for one night to share the news of the forest.

BLUEPAW SPEAKS:
My First Sight of Fourtrees

From the moment you take your first pawsteps outside the nursery, you long to go to Fourtrees. You long to meet cats from other Clans, to gaze up at Great Rock beneath StarClan. But you have to wait. Six moons, to be exact, until you're an apprentice.

My first Gathering was only two days after I received my apprentice name, Bluepaw. In my first training session, I caught a squirrel that was as big as me. My mentor, Stonepelt, was so impressed, he invited me to the Gathering, ahead of the older apprentices.

The moon was as round and yellow as my mother Moonflower's

eyes. She ran beside me, her tail lifted proudly. We stopped at the top of a wooded slope. I gazed down into a wide clearing. At each corner of the clearing was a tree—four massive oaks that looked as old as the Highstones beyond.

The clearing was full of cats, meowing and murmuring. In the moonlight, their fur looked silver, and it rippled like the surface of the river. Their eyes flashed like leaping fish. In the center of the clearing stood the Great Rock. It seemed to grow out of the earth, like the peak of a mountain whose roots spread beneath the whole forest.

My fur tingled as I scrambled down into Fourtrees for the first time. I vowed that one day I'd be the one leading ThunderClan in a flurry of fur and claws into the clearing. I'd be the one who leaped onto the Great Rock with the other Clan leaders. One day, I would be Bluestar, leader of ThunderClan.

HIGHSTONES

far to the north of WindClan's territory, across a dangerous Thunderpath, there is a range of mountains known to the cats as Highstones. Deep inside a cave in the mountain lies the Moonstone, a glowing rock turned to silver by the moonlight. This is where cats from all the Clans must go to communicate with StarClan. Leaders travel here to receive their nine lives and their warrior name. Medicine cats visit the Moonstone together once a month at the half-moon, to trade remedies and share tongues with StarClan.

HOW THE MOONSTONE
WAS DISCOVERED

Many moons ago, at the dawn of the forest, Clan leaders had no way of sharing tongues with their warrior ancestors. Spirits appeared to them in dreams, but they had no way of seeking guidance.

At this time, there was a WindClan cat named Mothflight. She had soft white fur and stormy green eyes. Her paws were swift, and her heart was true, but she was restless, easily distracted, and forgetful. She would return from hunting patrols with berries instead of prey. When asked what the berries were for, she would say she didn't know, but she thought they might be useful.

More than once, the WindClan deputy, Gorsefur, found Mothflight nosing at plants over the border in other Clans' territories. If she was caught by cats from another Clan, Gorsefur knew that WindClan would pay the price.

One morning, Windstar was leading a patrol along the edge of the Thunderpath. She felt the rumble of a Twoleg monster beneath her paws and glanced back at her warriors. Her breath caught in her throat.

Mothflight was crossing the Thunderpath, following a light blue feather as it drifted over into ShadowClan territory.

"Mothflight!"

The WindClan leader's yowl was drowned out by the monster's roar as Gorsefur dashed across the Thunderpath, shoving Mothflight to safety on the far side. Gravel spat into their faces as the monster rumbled past, trailing foul-smelling smoke.

"Stay here," Windstar hissed to the rest of the patrol, and sped across the Thunderpath. She was furious. Gorsefur was not just her deputy; he was the father of her kits.

"Mouse-brain!" Windstar growled at the white warrior. "Stargazing, feather-watching, hollow-headed mouse-brain! You could have been killed—you could *both* have been killed!"

Mothflight scuffled her paws in the dirt. "I'm sorry, Windstar," she meowed. "I felt like it was calling to me."

"The feather?" Windstar meowed. "Calling you where?"

Mothflight nodded at a ridge of jagged stone peaks in the distance, far beyond any Clan territory.

"Very well then," Windstar meowed. "Follow your feathers, stuff your head with clouds, eat nothing but berries as far as I care. If you cannot devote yourself to the warrior code, we cannot trust you in our Clan. You must go."

Mothflight's face fell. "But I belong to WindClan!"

"This is your punishment, Mothflight." Windstar's eyes were cold as the north wind.

Heavy with sorrow, Mothflight left her home. She walked all day, crossing out of ShadowClan territory, toward the teethlike rocks. As she climbed higher, the grass below her paws became bare, rocky soil, and the trees were replaced by boulders as large as the Great Rock at Fourtrees. The sun sank behind the ridge, turning the rocks to sharp black fangs.

Mothflight was licking her scratched paws when a thrush burst out of a bush, flying low to the ground. She tore after it, then came skidding to a halt around a large boulder. Mothflight barely noticed as the bird escaped into the orange sky. She was staring at the mountain in front of her, where a large, square hole yawned in the rock face.

Cautiously she padded up to the opening. It was completely dark inside, black and silent like a gaping mouth. Outside, the shadows were lengthening. She would be an easy target for night predators. She sniffed the black air inside the tunnel; it did not smell of other animals.

Mothflight padded into the mouth of the cave, feeling the cold stone under her paws. She crept forward, feeling the tunnel narrow and wind downward. Sometimes she became aware of other passages going off in other directions, but something drew her on. In the cold black air she felt dizzy and light, as if she were made of clouds. Her tail brushed the roof of the tunnel. But she traveled deeper into the mountain, unafraid.

She didn't know how long she had been walking when a new scent drifted into her nostrils. It smelled like fresh air and prey. Mothflight stopped. A silvery light was trickling into the darkness in front of her, revealing a glittering cavern. High in the roof, she saw a triangle of night sky and then the climbing moon. It poured its bright silver light through the hole onto a stone at the center of the cave.

The stone was three tail-lengths high, and it glittered like raindrops on cobwebs. Mothflight crept forward, her fur tingling. Following an instinct she didn't understand, she lay down, closed her eyes, and pressed her nose against the cold surface of the stone. Then she opened her eyes. The cave was filled with shimmering cats.

"Welcome, Mothflight. You have found the Moonstone," one of the spirits murmured. "It is a sacred place. You must take the knowledge of this place back to the forest cats."

"But I can't!" Mothflight blurted. "I've been exiled." She hung her head.

"You were exiled precisely for the strengths we need," meowed the spirit. "Your curiosity, your visions, your openness to the signs in the world. We choose you to be the first medicine cat."

Mothflight's heart filled with a strange, fierce joy. "What does that mean?"

"You will devote yourself to your Clan," meowed another spirit. "You will learn the ways of healing herbs. You will read the omens we send you to advise your leader on difficult questions and keep your Clan safe."

Mothflight shook her head. "Windstar will never let me return."

"Is that true, Windstar?"

Mothflight spun around to see the shadowy figure of her leader.

"You are dreaming, Windstar," whispered the spirit. "Welcome your new medicine cat. She will return to you."

Windstar's ears twitched, and her fur flattened. She looked into Mothflight's green eyes, nodded, and vanished into the air.

"These are the cats you must find," another voice meowed. Three cats appeared before her, each of them curled in a sleeping ball.

"Dapplepelt, from RiverClan," purred one starry cat, padding up to a delicate tortoiseshell.

"Pebbleheart, from ShadowClan," whispered another, prodding a dark gray tabby until he snarled in his sleep.

"And Cloudspots, from ThunderClan." The first spirit pointed his tail at a long-furred black cat with white ears, a white chest, and two white paws.

"Bring them here at the next half-moon," the spirit-cats meowed, "and we will teach you all how to be medicine cats."

As they faded away, leaving only the glitter of stars, Mothflight stretched and tucked herself into a comfortable ball. Tonight she would sleep beside the Moonstone. Tomorrow, she would return to the forest as the first medicine cat of the Clans.

THE MOONPOOL

When the warrior Clans arrived at their new home by the lake, they knew they needed to find a replacement for the Moonstone. Highstones was too far to travel, and the cats needed guidance from StarClan. The ThunderClan medicine cat apprentice, Leafpaw, was the one who found the Moonpool. This small pool high in the hills above WindClan is surrounded by stone walls and fed by a trickling waterfall. Ancient pawprints in the stone suggest that other cats came to this sacred place once, a long time ago. . . .

AN ANCIENT CAT SPEAKS

My name is Rock. Many generations past, my kin lived on the lakeshore. Now new cats have come here and walk in our pawprints. They have brought their own warrior ancestors with them. Their fur brushes mine as they learn the sky paths I have trodden for seasons.

They live in four Clans, unlike our three Tribes that scattered so long ago. They have a separate medicine cat and leader, unlike our healers, who were both. And they have found the Moonpool, the place of the ancestors. The pool is as round as the full moon.

I used to travel to the Moonpool with the two other healers. Then we followed the stream up to its source, high in the hills, and onward to a deep claw-slice in the hills. At the far end, we climbed a steep, rocky slope to a stream beyond.

We followed the stream up to a barrier of thornbushes. Once inside, we would stand for a short while, looking down at the hollow and listening to the sound of the water bubbling out of the sheer cliff beyond.

In the center of the hollow is the Moonpool.

We knew the path that spiraled down to it like the scent of our own Tribes. Then we closed our eyes, drank from the water's edge, and waited for the visions to appear. I remember the clear, cold taste of the water, like drinking silver moonlight.

It gives me joy to see new tribes traveling to the Moonpool. I hope it will bring them serenity, wisdom, and guidance for many moons to come.

THE ISLAND

In their new home by the lake, the Clans also needed a replacement for Fourtrees—a place to hold the peaceful monthly Gathering. At first they met by the Twoleg horse-place, but a better spot was soon found. The Island is just off the shore of RiverClan territory. It would be impossible for young cats and elders to swim to, but StarClan made a tree fall across the span of the water. Now the cats use the tree as a bridge to get to the Island every full moon. There they can meet in safety, on neutral, sacred ground.

DUSTPELT SPEAKS:
How StarClan Gave Us a New Gathering Place

When we first arrived at the lake, I remember looking down from the hill and seeing a dark shape on the near end, and I thought to myself, *Dustpelt, that's an island!* I said so to Ferncloud, although she doesn't remember it now.

Hawkfrost said it would be a perfect place for the RiverClan camp. Imagine! One Clan taking the whole Island! And anyway, how would their kits and elders manage the swim from the lakeshore? But StarClan had other plans. They wanted the Island to be the place of Gatherings, a neutral place for the Clans to meet, like Fourtrees.

A huge storm blew in. Mudclaw tried to snatch the leadership of WindClan away from Onewhisker, but we chased him off, down to the lakeshore. Then a bolt of fire struck a tree on the Island and brought it crashing down on the lakeside, crushing Mudclaw. Onewhisker was the rightful leader of WindClan, and to prove it, StarClan had sent us a way to get to the Island for Gatherings.

Now every full moon, the Gathering takes place in the clearing at the center of the Island, surrounded by bushes and trees. The leaders look down on all the Clans from the branches of a tree, with their deputies on the roots below.

It's a strong and safe place. And best of all, it belongs to all the Clans now.

SUN-DROWN-PLACE

Not far from the Clan's new lakeside home, there is a vast expanse of water known as the sun-drown-place. Here the sun sinks into the sea every night as if it were being swallowed up. The water is strangely salty and roars as it beats the shore. This is where Midnight the badger lives. This is where the questing cats were sent to learn that the Clans had to leave the forest and travel to a new home.

TAWNYPELT SPEAKS:
Journey's End

I could barely lift my paws to follow the others. The air was filled with the smell of salt, and beneath the shrieking of strange birds I could hear a distant roaring sound. I thought the giant cats of LionClan were prowling out of sight.

Then we reached the top of a cliff, and there below us was a sandy slope stretching down to the water. I didn't know there was room in the world for so much water. We couldn't even see the end of it. It was frothing and roaring and leaping up onto the sand. The sun was a flame-red ball on the horizon; we watched it sink into the water, leaving the world dark.

Brambleclaw led the way along the cliff, which slanted closer to the water the farther we went. The edge of the cliff was jagged. I could see the frothing water through cracks in the rock. It was through one of these cracks that Brambleclaw fell, with Squirrelpaw and me tumbling after him.

The salty water got into our mouths and stung our eyes. It wanted to drag us away. But we swam to dry ground. This was the cave we'd been looking for.

Of course, Feathertail found a better way down, using a series of ledges along the cliff wall. That's how Midnight gets in and out. Who's Midnight? Oh, she's a badger. But we'll get to her story later. . . .

CEREMONIES

LEADERS

Clan leaders are the heart of the Clan; their personality affects how the Clan operates and how their warriors treat one another and the world around them. It is up to the Clan leaders to set a good example and guide their Clanmates along the path of the warrior code. They are responsible for calling Clan meetings, appointing warriors, mentors, and apprentices, and deciding Clan policy and strategy with the help of their deputy and any cats they choose to consult for advice (usually the medicine cat, the elders, or senior warriors).

When a cat becomes Clan leader, he or she must travel to the Moonstone (or after the Clans moved to the lake, the Moonpool) and share tongues with the warrior ancestors of StarClan. The Clan's medicine cat accompanies them on the journey but leaves them alone for the ceremony, in which the leader is granted eight extra lives and a new name with "star" at the end (Bluestar, Firestar, etc.).

This process can be surprising and painful, but it is important for leaders to be able to fight fiercely for their Clan and live long enough to pass along their wisdom and prepare a new leader. During the ceremony, each life is given to the new leader by a cat whose life was significant to the new leader in some way (see *Firestar's Nine Lives*).

When a leader loses a life, she or he blacks out for a short period of time, during which that cat visits StarClan and speaks with its warrior ancestors. On returning to consciousness, the leader must still recover from the injury or illness that felled him or her. Medicine cats can usually tell how many lives a leader has left, although the number is kept secret from rival Clans.

FIRESTAR'S NINE LIVES

LIONHEART The brave former ThunderClan deputy gave Firestar a life with the gift of courage, to defend his Clan in battle.

REDTAIL Firestar ever met Bluestar's first deputy, but he worked hard to uncover the truth about Redtail's murder. For this reason, Redtail gave him a life with the gift of justice, to judge his Clanmates fairly.

SILVERSTREAM The beautiful RiverClan tabby, the love of Graystripe's life, gave Fireheart the gift of loyalty to what he knows to be right. This understanding would guide him even beyond the reach of the warrior code.

RUNNINGWIND The swift ThunderClan warrior presented his life with the gift of tireless energy, so Firestar could serve his Clan to the utmost.

BRINDLEFACE With this life, Brindleface gave Firestar the same desire to protect his

Clan that a mother has for her kits. He expected this to be a warm, nurturing feeling, but instead he felt it as the fiercest anger burning in his claws, ready to slash and kill to defend his Clanmates.

SWIFTPAW This young apprentice strayed from the Clan into the jaws of a dog pack. He gave Firestar the gift of mentoring.

YELLOWFANG Compassion was Yellowfang's gift, the compassion of a medicine cat for all those who need her help. It is an important gift for a leader, who must be mindful of cats weaker than himself.

SPOTTEDLEAF With her life, the young medicine cat gave Firestar love, signaling her approval of his love for Sandstorm.

BLUESTAR Firestar's leader and mentor gave him his last life, along with the gifts of nobility, certainty, and faith, so that he would be able to lead his Clan in the way of the warrior code for all nine of his lives.

DEPUTIES

"I say these words before the body of Redtail,
so that his spirit may hear and approve my choice.
Lionheart will be the new deputy
of ThunderClan."

A Clan's deputy is chosen by the leader, to assist in taking care of the Clan. To qualify, a warrior must have had an apprentice and must be strong and brave, with the qualities needed to take on leadership of the Clan if necessary.

The deputy presides over Clan meetings when the leader is absent, stands in for the leader at Gatherings if the leader is ill, organizes daily patrols, and oversees the training of apprentices. According to the warrior code, when a deputy dies or steps down, the leader must announce a new deputy before moonhigh.

Deputies stop being deputies if:

- ❖ the Clan leader dies, leaving the deputy to take over as leader.
- ❖ the deputy retires and becomes an elder.
- ❖ the deputy commits a crime against the warrior code and is demoted or driven from the Clan.
- ❖ the deputy dies or is killed in battle.

APPRENTICES

*"By naming apprentices, we show that
ThunderClan will survive and remain strong.
Birchkit, from now on you will be known as Birchpaw. . . .
Ashfur, you are ready for an apprentice.
You will be Birchpaw's mentor."*

Before a cat can become a warrior, he or she must be trained to fight and hunt and defend the Clan. At the age of six moons, kits leave the nursery and become apprentices. At this point they change the second half of their name from "kit" to "paw" to symbolize the path their paws are now on. The Clan leader assigns each apprentice a mentor—an older warrior to guide the apprentice on the path to being a warrior. Apprentices are responsible for chores around the camp, such as tending to the elders, in addition to their training. If they work hard, listen to their mentors, and live by the warrior code, soon they will earn their warrior name, and hopefully, one day, the chance to be a mentor themselves.

BIRCHPAW SPEAKS:
A New Apprentice

I can't believe I'm finally an apprentice. I've been dreaming of this for moons! It's true my mother, Ferncloud, wouldn't have minded keeping me in the nursery a while longer. She still licks me as if I were a tiny kit sometimes. But I know she misses Larchkit and Hollykit, who died when the forest ran out of prey, and she worries about me, so I let her.

I'm lucky to have Ashfur as my mentor. He's smart and patient and lets me practice everything instead of just showing me how to do it.

I love hunting patrols the best. We can't eat anything until we've brought back enough food for the elders, but it's so exciting to jump on a mouse, or chase a squirrel, or sneak up on a starling. I've heard stories about apprentices who ate while they were supposed to be hunting and how much trouble they got in. That's not going to happen to me!

I can't wait for my first Gathering, when we are allowed to talk in peace with cats from other Clans. I hope to see Toadkit, Marshkit, and Applekit there. They're ShadowClan cats, but we became friends on the journey from the forest. Maybe I'll tell them that the thrush I nearly caught was actually an eagle. They'd be so impressed!

WARRIORS

"Brackenpaw, you warned the Clan today,
and you fought bravely in the battle," Bluestar meowed.
"It is time for you to become a warrior."

Warriors are the lifeblood of the Clan. They patrol the borders, keep the fresh-kill pile supplied, and defend their Clanmates against attacks from enemy cats or predators. They fight to protect the Clan for as long as they are able and are often called upon to mentor apprentices, passing on the skills they were taught. During the warrior naming ceremony, an apprentice gives up the "paw" half of his or her name and earns a real warrior name—such as Fireheart, Sandstorm, or Brambleclaw.

BRACKENFUR SPEAKS:
A New Warrior

Iremember the day I became a warrior. I was stretching outside the apprentices' den when Fireheart asked if I wanted to go hunting with him. I don't know where my own mentor was—Graystripe seemed very busy in those days.

When I smelled the WindClan and ShadowClan cats, I knew our camp was in danger because of Brokentail. Back when I was a kit and he was leader of ShadowClan, he stole me and my brother and sisters from ThunderClan. He was driven out and exiled from ShadowClan, but then he led a rogue attack on the ThunderClan camp. Now he was a ThunderClan prisoner, and the other Clans didn't like it one bit. That's why they were coming to attack us.

Fireheart sent me back to camp to warn Bluestar and Tigerclaw. I knew they were coming for Brokentail, so I planted myself outside his den and fought as hard as I could. It was strange fighting to defend such an evil cat. But I knew Bluestar wanted us to defend him. That's what loyalty to the Clan is all about.

After we drove off the invaders, Bluestar made me a warrior. The whole Clan called out my warrior name, Brackenfur. I felt their support and love, and I was so proud of my actions and my choices.

That's what I thought about during my silent vigil. After the ceremony, I wasn't allowed to speak to any cat until dawn. I guarded the camp alone, though I was tired from the battle. I looked up at the twinkling lights of Silverpelt and felt StarClan watching me. It was comforting to know that even when my Clanmates left this life, they'd watch over me, until the day I joined StarClan as well.

When Firestar gave me Whitepaw to mentor, he talked about how I'd learned about strength and friendship from Graystripe and how he hoped I'd pass on that loyalty and determination to her. Whitepaw is eager to learn and excited. I take her on boundary patrol whenever I can, renewing the scent markings and checking for signs of trespassers. We hunt for food for the elders and the queens, and I'm teaching her to climb trees and jump as high as she can to catch flying birds.

Soon, she will become a warrior. I can't wait to see her eyes shine as Firestar says her warrior name and to share in her happiness with the rest of the Clan.

FIGHTING TECHNIQUES

One of the most important skills a mentor must teach an apprentice is how to fight. Warriors are often called upon to defend the borders or protect the Clan from attack, whether by enemy Clans or predators like badgers and foxes. Even medicine cats must learn enough fighting technique to be useful in battle.

Back kick Explosive surprise move to catch opponent from behind. Judge opponent's distance from you carefully; then lash out with your back legs, taking your weight on your front paws.

Belly rake A fight-stopper. Slice with unsheathed claws across soft flesh of opponent's belly. If you're pinned down, the belly rake quickly puts you back in control.

Front paw blow Frontal attack. Bring your front paw down hard on your opponent's head. Claws sheathed.

Front paw strike Frontal attack. Slice downward with your front paw at the body or face of your opponent. Claws unsheathed.

Killing bite A death blow to the back of the neck. Quick and silent and sometimes considered dishonorable. Used only as a last resort.

Leap-and-hold Ideal for a small cat facing a large opponent. Spring onto opponent's back and grip with unsheathed claws. Now you are beyond the range of your opponent's paws and in position to inflict severe body wounds. A group of apprentices can defeat a large and dangerous warrior in this way. It was deployed to great effect against BloodClan's deputy, Bone. Watch for the drop-and-roll countermove, and try to jump free before you get squashed.

Partner fighting Warriors who have trained and fought together will often instinctively fall into a paired defensive position, each protecting the other's back while fending off an opponent on either side. Slashing, clawing, and leaping together, battle pairs can be a whirlwind of danger for attackers.

Play dead Effective in a tight situation, such as when you are pinned. Stop struggling and go limp. When your opponent relaxes his grip, thinking you are defeated, push yourself up explosively. This will throw off an unwary opponent and put you in an attacking position.

Scruff shake Secure a strong teeth grip in the scruff of your opponent's neck; then shake violently until he or she is too rattled to fight back. Most effective against rats, which are small enough to throw. A strong throw will stun or kill them.

Teeth grip Target your opponent's extremities—the legs, tail, scruff, or ears—and sink in your teeth and hold. This move is similar to the leap-and-hold except your claws remain free to fight.

Upright lock Final, crushing move on already weakened opponent. Rear up on back legs and bring full weight down on opponent. If opponent does same, wrestle and flip him under you. This move makes you vulnerable to the belly rake, so requires great strength and speed.

ELDERS

*"Goldenflower, is it your wish to give up
the name of warrior and go to join the elders?"
"It is."
"Your Clan honors you and all the service
you have given us. I call upon StarClan to give
you many seasons of rest."*

The life of a warrior is difficult and dangerous, and many die young—in battle, of disease, or from a natural disaster. Those cats lucky enough to live a long life may eventually retire from their warrior duties to become elders. These elderly cats are viewed with the deepest respect by the rest of the Clan. Many moons of experience make them an invaluable source of advice for the Clan leader, and they keep alive Clan history by passing down the old stories.

GOLDENFLOWER SPEAKS:
A New Role to Play

As a young apprentice, I dreamed of being a warrior, and I wondered what it would be like to have kits. But I never thought about becoming an elder. Now I know I am lucky to have made it this far.

All the cats treat elders with respect. Even apprentices listen to me; I can't say they always did when I was a warrior. We elders spend our days peacefully, for the most part—discussing the goings-on in the forest, telling stories about the old days, or just snoozing in the sun.

Don't get me wrong. I still have plenty of fight left. I'd be ready to hunt or defend the camp in an instant. When I was a queen nursing Swiftkit, an elder named Rosetail died defending us from a ShadowClan attack. I would do the same for our nursery kits today.

There is one sad duty we elders perform. When a cat dies, all Clan cats gather for a final vigil. We share tongues and groom our Clanmate one last time. That night certain cats lie beside the body in mourning—its family, mentor, apprentice, and littermates. At dawn, we elders are the ones who take the body out of the camp for burial.

So it has always been. I've served my Clan for a long time, and it's nice to finally have some peace and quiet. I hope I get to stick around and enjoy it for many moons to come.

BREAKING THE WARRIOR CODE

❖

CLOUDTAIL SPEAKS:
Tempted by the Kittypet Life

I didn't mean to break the warrior code. I just didn't understand it. Parts of it seemed stupid to me, so I figured I should just follow the smart parts. And Fireheart never stopped to explain *why* I had to follow these rules. He was too busy pointing out the things I did wrong instead of the things I did right. I was faster than Brightpaw, stronger than Thornpaw, and smarter than Swiftpaw and Ashpaw put together. I was determined to show the Clan that I could be a great warrior, even though I was born a kittypet.

One day, I caught a pigeon just before it took off. Instead of praising my skill, Fireheart scolded me like a wayward kit. He said I didn't respect my prey.

I was fed up with Fireheart's lectures, so I ran off. He could have chased me, but he didn't. I ran until I smelled the Thunderpath, and I knew I had reached Twolegplace. I thought about visiting my mother, but I was too worked up, so I decided to explore.

I saw a plump black-and-white tom sunning himself on top of a fence, and a long-haired gray cat chasing a butterfly in circles. It looked more fun than hunting for elders or sparring with Fireheart, so on I went.

I was just passing a pale green fence when a gate opened. It nearly scared my whiskers off! A Twoleg female stood over me, and when she saw me, she crouched down and made this odd cooing noise. I flattened my ears and hissed, and to my surprise, the Twoleg went back through the fence, leaving the gate open. Had I scared her off? I poked my nose inside to see. The grass was short, with flowery bushes around the edges. I watched the Twoleg climb some steps and go through the door of her nest. Then, the door opened again, and the Twoleg set something down on the steps. I waited until she had gone back inside; then I crept forward to investigate. It smelled delicious, like fish, only heartier and less slimy. It was pink and sitting on top of a hard white leaf. Next to it was another leaf, filled with something white that brought back memories of the nursery. I realized it was milk.

Before I knew it, I'd eaten and drunk it all. I was hungry! And besides, I couldn't take it back to the elders. I wasn't hurting anyone. I knew the warrior code said that we shouldn't let ourselves live like kittypets. But I didn't see why we should reject free food. It left more in the forest for everyone else, right? And it was so easy.

I started going nearly every day, whenever I could slip off. Soon the Twoleg let me come inside, where I saw a Twoleg male clomping about. They had a small, yippy white dog. It tried to play with me at first, but it wasn't dangerous. It was barely smart enough to walk.

Mostly I got hard brown pellets to eat, instead of the yummy pink stuff, but they didn't taste bad. I didn't even mind the stale water.

Sometimes I wondered why my mother had sent me away from this life. But I didn't mean to stay. I still wanted to be a warrior. I just thought I could have both. Well, I learned the hard way that I was wrong.

When the Twolegs caught me and put me in a wire web inside the belly of a monster, I thought that ThunderClan would be pleased to see the last of the kittypets. But I still wanted them to know that I had been taken against my will. Deep down, I was a ThunderClan cat. I wanted my warrior ceremony. I wanted to be admired as a great hunter and fighter. I wanted to go to Gatherings. And I'll tell you a secret . . . I was already a little bit in love with Brightpaw.

Fireheart said StarClan led him to me, but I think it was luck that I ran into his friend Ravenpaw near the Twolegs' new nest. Either way, when I saw Fireheart through the window, it felt like all of LionClan had come to rescue me. I was so happy that ThunderClan wanted me back.

Fireheart was angry, of course. But Sandstorm was nice about it. Ashpaw was excited to see me again, and the elders loved hearing the story of my capture; I couldn't help exaggerating a bit. I loved the way they thought I had been on some heroic quest instead of misbehaving.

After all that, I knew better than to go near Twolegs again. And I realized there were parts of the warrior code that I might not understand but that were there for a reason. Seeing my Clanmates listen to my story so eagerly made me want to be a warrior, like Fireheart, who really was a hero.

More than anything, I wanted to be a loyal ThunderClan warrior.

CROWFEATHER SPEAKS:
A Forbidden Love

Have you ever loved another cat so much it made your heart ache and your fur tremble?

Feathertail understood me, and she listened to me. Her eyes were the clear blue of her river home. She died saving us all from Sharpclaw. After that, I wanted only to serve my Clan to the limits of my strength, and then to join Feathertail in StarClan.

But then I met Leafpaw. She was patient and kind. Her voice was like water flowing over pebbles, and her scent had hints of wildflowers in it.

What was happening to me? How could I fall in love with anyone—let alone a ThunderClan cat—let alone a ThunderClan medicine cat? I know the warrior code! I've always been a loyal WindClan cat. I knew that if I let myself fall for her, it could endanger my Clan. If my loyalties were divided, how could I be a true warrior? How could I defend WindClan against a ThunderClan attack, knowing that I might hurt her or someone Leafpaw loves?

And medicine cats are especially forbidden to fall in love. She cannot be thinking of me instead of her Clanmates—they depend on her too much. And StarClan might have trouble reaching her if her thoughts were all wound up in me. I knew they would be very angry with us. I wished I could fall in love with a WindClan she-cat—I wished I could feel this way without breaking the warrior code. But there is no cat in WindClan like Leafpaw.

I thought that when we reached the lake and went our separate ways I'd be able to forget her. But first she came to our camp to bring watermint to our sick cats, Morningflower and Darkfoot. And the way I felt when I saw her—it made me angry to realize how little I could control my feelings. Onewhisker asked me to escort her home. I went as fast as I could; if I spoke to her, my secret might come spilling out. As I left her camp, Leafpaw thanked me in this sweet, natural way, as if I hadn't been behaving like a badger with its fur clawed off. I had to get out of there before every cat could see what I was trying so hard to fight.

After Leafpaw found the Moonpool, she brought me a message from Feathertail. She said I should stop grieving and open my eyes to the living. What did that mean? Could Feathertail approve of my love for Leafpaw? Wasn't she angry?

It was raining the night everything changed. Onewhisker was planning to travel to the Moonpool to receive his nine lives. I'd noticed Mudclaw's whispers and looks, but I never thought he'd try anything so reckless as attack to Onewhisker—and bring other Clans to help him too!

As the battle was breaking up, Brambleclaw sent me chasing after two ShadowClan cats who made a run for it. We tore across the moors and into the ThunderClan woods. Branches whipped at my face, and rain sliced through my fur, but I ran on, determined to catch the traitors and punish them for all the wrongs done to my Clan.

I heard yowling ahead of me, and I crashed through some bushes, and there she was. The two ShadowClan warriors had fallen to their deaths, but Leafpaw was clinging desperately to the edge of a cliff, her claws scrabbling on the slick, wet rock. Her wild amber eyes met mine, and she called for help. I was frozen. . . . All I could think of was how I had failed Feathertail, how she had died because I couldn't save her.

But I saved Leafpaw. She brought me back. She helped me shake off the memories as I reached forward and pulled her to safety. We lay there on the ground, gasping for breath, and I knew in that moment that I couldn't fight my feelings anymore. I loved Leafpaw, and I told her so.

From the look in her eyes, I knew she felt the same way. She said everything I'd been feeling—that this couldn't happen, that she was a medicine cat. But I could see her heart blazing in the depths of her eyes. I could see how much she cared for me too. I'd seen the same look in Feathertail's eyes . . . but this was different. This was more dangerous, more forbidden. There was a feeling like lightning prickling along my fur every time I looked at Leafpaw. And now I knew she felt it too.

I decided at that moment that we would find a way to be together. The future was terrifying, but we would face it together . . . our pelts brushing, our tails twined. Our hearts in love, forever.

pROphecIes aNd OMeNs

StarClan's messages are not always clear. Perhaps the hardest part of a medicine cat's job is reading the omens that are hidden in the natural world. Do they truly come from StarClan? What do they mean? How can they guide our pawsteps?

It is easy to misread their meanings or to manipulate how they are read. For instance, RiverClan's medicine cat, Mudfur, found a moth's wing lying outside his den, which he took to be a sign that Mothwing should be his apprentice, even though she was the daughter of a rogue cat and Tigerstar. However, as Leafpool later discovered, Mothwing's brother Hawkfrost actually left the moth's wing there on purpose, intending to trick Mudfur into believing it was a sign. His plan succeeded, paving the way for Hawkfrost to blackmail his sister into manipulating future signs to his benefit as well.

Some cats see signs everywhere; others doubt that StarClan is behind them. If our spirit ancestors can walk in our dreams and speak with us, why would they need to use such cryptic messages?

But there have been some undeniable omens. Before the battle with BloodClan, Firestar saw instead of his own reflection the face of a lion in a pool. He realized this was a reference to the lion and tiger prophecy (see *Major Prophecies*) and that only by combining the four Clans into LionClan could he save the forest.

As WindClan returned from their exile, the WindClan medicine cat, Barkface, saw the dawn clouds stained with blood. He interpreted that the day would bring an unnecessary death. It was true. On their way back to the ThunderClan camp, Fireheart and Graystripe were attacked by a RiverClan patrol, and a warrior named Whiteclaw fell to his death over the edge of the Gorge.

Prophecies, on the other hand, are proclamations from StarClan that foretell huge events in the future of the Clans. Although they may seem ominous and hard to understand, they mark significant turning points in the span of Clan history.

MAJOR PROPHECIES

BLUESTAR SPEAKS:
Fire Alone Can Save Our Clan

Spottedleaf received this message from StarClan on the night of the battle at Sunningrocks. It was my first defeat as ThunderClan's leader. Morale was low, and there were stirrings of trouble from ShadowClan. ThunderClan needed more warriors, and I needed a sign from StarClan. But what we got didn't make sense.

"Fire alone can save our Clan."

But fire is feared by all the Clans. How could it save us?

A few days later, I was leading a patrol along the edge of the woods near Twolegplace. Tigerclaw had gone on ahead with Ravenpaw, and I was turning to ask Redtail a question when I spotted a cat sitting on a fence, looking out at the forest. From the way he held himself, I thought he must be a Clan cat. He looked proud and restless and curious, ready to charge into battle. A ray of sunshine broke through the clouds and touched his orange pelt. It lit up like a blaze of flame. In the next instant, the clouds closed in, and the fire dimmed; the cat began washing his paws with quick, delicate strokes. I realized he was just a kittypet—the prophecy must have muddled my brain. A kittypet would be about as much use to us as fire!

Still, I kept thinking about him, and I wasn't surprised when we ran into him again on a patrol. Lionheart and I saw him hunting a mouse. He had excellent form and sharp eyes. When Graypaw attacked him, rather than running like a regular kittypet, he turned to defend himself.

Maybe there was something to my theory after all. . . .

That's why I invited him to join the Clan. That's why I named him Firepaw—part of me was hoping that he was a cat of prophecy and destiny.

And I was right.

When I died and joined StarClan, I knew that Fireheart had saved ThunderClan many times over and would do so again as leader. He is living fire: he has the warmth of fire to protect his Clan and the ferocity of fire to defend it.

FIRESTAR SPEAKS:
Four Will Become Two, Lion and Tiger Will Meet in Battle, and Blood Will Rule the Forest

This prophecy came to me during my leadership ceremony. I had received my nine lives and my Clan leader name. Then, even as StarClan welcomed me, I saw a hill of bones spattered with blood. I heard Bluestar whisper, "Something terrible is coming, Firestar. Four will become two. Lion and tiger will meet in battle, and blood will rule the forest."

The meaning of the prophecy revealed itself to me gradually. Four will become two—that meant the forest Clans. RiverClan joined ShadowClan under Tigerstar's leadership, calling themselves TigerClan. ThunderClan joined WindClan to make LionClan . . . two Clans where there used to be four. Then lion and tiger would meet in battle.

I had no way of knowing about BloodClan, of course, until Tigerstar revealed his alliance with Scourge. That's when I discovered our real enemy. LionClan and TigerClan had to unite to drive out Scourge, or else Blood really would rule the forest.

Luckily I had something Scourge did not—faith in StarClan. With my nine lives and my warrior ancestors fighting beside me, I defeated BloodClan.

In the end, peace, not blood, ruled the forest.

BRAMBLECLAW SPEAKS:

Darkness, Air, Water, and Sky Will Come Together and Shake the Forest to Its Roots

This prophecy came to me, Brambleclaw, not to a medicine cat or a leader. Bluestar, the former ThunderClan leader, told me in a dream that I had to meet with three other cats at the new moon and listen to midnight.

Have you ever heard anything more peculiar? Who were these cats, where were we supposed to meet, and how could midnight tell us anything?

I learned the full prophecy later, after much traveling and danger. "Darkness, air, water, and sky will come together and shake the forest to its roots. Nothing will be as it is now, nor as it has been before."

Can you guess what this meant? It meant that four cats from each Clan would come together. ShadowClan was darkness, WindClan was air, RiverClan was water, and ThunderClan was sky. We did shake the forest to its roots, but we had no choice. The Twolegs were destroying our home with their monsters. There was no safe way for cats to live in the forest anymore. Tawnypelt, Crowpaw, Feathertail, and I were chosen to lead our Clanmates to a new home.

That's what StarClan meant when they said, "Nothing will be as it is now, nor as it has been before." From the moment we set paw outside the forest, with the cats of all four Clans following us, I knew that wherever we went and wherever we settled, nothing could ever be the same.

LEAFPOOL SPEAKS:
Before There Is Peace, Blood Will Spill Blood, and the Lake Will Run Red

This prophecy came to me on our first night in the new camp, in a dream. I am Leafpool, the ThunderClan medicine cat. In my dream, I was gazing at the stars reflected on the lake when the water turned bloodred. Then I heard a voice whisper, *"Before there is peace, blood will spill blood, and the lake will run red."*

I knew it meant that there would be bloodshed before there could be peace. But what could I do about it? And when would it happen?

When Mudclaw and Hawkfrost rose up against Onewhisker, I wondered if that was the event in the prophecy. Later, I thought it might be the badger attack. But the prophecy kept returning to my dreams.

I knew that Brambleclaw was meeting his father, Tigerstar, in his dreams, and, of course, I was afraid of where that might lead. So when I heard that Firestar was in mortal danger, I thought he had been betrayed by Brambleclaw. I blamed myself for not having warned my father in time.

But I was wrong.

Brambleclaw's brother, Hawkfrost, had set a trap for Firestar. Brambleclaw had fought and killed Hawkfrost to protect his leader. That's what the prophecy meant by "blood will spill blood"—the death of Hawkfrost at the paws of his brother.

As Hawkfrost's blood spilled into the lake, turning the water red, I knew that I could never fight a cat of my own blood. I couldn't imagine how Brambleclaw must be feeling.

At least now, I thought, there can finally be peace.

MEDICINE

MEDICINE CATS

"Leafpaw, do you promise to uphold
the ways of a medicine cat, to stand apart from the rivalry
between Clan and Clan, and to protect all cats equally,
even at the cost of your life?"
"I do."
"Then by the powers of StarClan I give you
your true name as a medicine cat. Leafpaw, from this
moment you will be known as Leafpool."

No Clan could survive without a medicine cat's knowledge of healing herbs and compassion for the sick. In addition, these cats have a spiritual responsibility. Their unusually strong connection to StarClan allows them to receive and interpret visions that can guide the Clan through dark times.

Most medicine cats are born to their destiny. From a young age, these special kits are drawn to the medicine cat den. They are fascinated by the herbs and often have strange dreams of their

own. A medicine cat can spot which kit would make a good apprentice. If the kit agrees, he or she is brought to the sacred space (the Moonstone or the Moonpool) and initiated into the ranks of medicine cats through a secret ceremony.

The life of a medicine cat is not easy, but it is very rewarding. Although medicine cats cannot have a mate or kits, they are beloved and respected by the whole Clan. They devote their lives to protecting their Clanmates in a way that ordinary warriors cannot. And they know that there is a special place waiting for them in StarClan.

LEAFPOOL SPEAKS:
Not Just About Herbs

I knew I wanted to be a medicine cat from the time I was a small kit. I watched Cinderpelt taking care of sick cats and checking on my mother in the nursery. *I* wanted to be that gentle, kind, and intelligent. I wanted to know how to heal and how to read the signs from StarClan. I couldn't imagine anything more important.

I knew that medicine cats can never have kits. But I didn't think about what that would mean for me. I didn't ever expect to fall in love.

Cinderpelt let me help her in her den even before I was an apprentice. My sister was disappointed that we didn't get to train together as apprentices, but she understood how important this was to me.

Cinderpelt took me to the Moonstone for the initiation ceremony when I became an apprentice. It's a secret ritual involving the medicine cats of all the Clans and also StarClan—I've never felt closer to StarClan than I did then. . . . It was amazing. There's another ritual when we earn our full medicine cat names. I really wish I could tell you about it, but I have not the words. In truth, my experience of these ceremonies is not that of every medicine cat, and for this reason we are forbidden to talk about it. Perhaps it's true that there are some secrets that should never be told.

That's the best and also the scariest thing about being a medicine cat. Knowing all the herbs and helping my sick Clanmates is wonderful too, but more than that, I know that StarClan is depending on me. I am the one who has to bring their messages to the Clan. I have to understand what they want us to do or else terrible things could befall us. I am my Clan's guardian, in a way.

My friend Mothwing is RiverClan's medicine cat, but she doesn't believe in StarClan. It makes me sad for her—she's missing the most important part of this life. And for a while StarClan had no way to communicate with her, which placed the whole Clan in danger. But now she has Willowpaw, her apprentice. StarClan can speak to her, and so the line of wisdom passed down from our ancestors can continue unbroken.

We get a lot of respect in our Clans, but there is a lot of responsibility too. If I make a mistake, a cat could die. This is why you too have to be careful with your own cat friends. I'm showing you this list of our medicines, but you mustn't try using them yourself. You are not a medicine cat. Out in the forest, we have to use whatever we find, but kittypets have something called a veterinarian to look after them. My friend Cody told me about this. The veterinarian is like a Twoleg medicine cat, as far as I can tell. They heal cats, but they have many more medicines to work with than we do. Don't try giving any sick cats these herbs—either come find me, or take them to the veterinarian. Trust me, they'll thank you for it!

IMPORTANT MEDICINES
AND THEIR USES

BORAGE LEAVES To be chewed and eaten. The plant can be distinguished by its small blue or pink star-shaped flowers and hairy leaves. Great for nursing queens as it helps increase their supply of milk. Also brings down fever.

BURDOCK ROOT A tall-stemmed, sharp-smelling thistle with dark leaves. A medicine cat must dig up the roots, wash off the dirt, and chew them into a pulp, which can be applied to rat bites. Cures infection.

CATMINT (also known as catnip) A delicious-smelling, leafy plant that's hard to find in the wild; often found growing in Twoleg gardens. The best remedy for greencough.

CHERVIL A sweet-smelling plant with large, spreading, fernlike leaves and small white flowers. The juice of the leaves can be used for infected wounds, and chewing the roots helps with bellyache.

COBWEB Spiderwebs can be found all over the forest; be careful not to bring along the spider when you take the web! Medicine cats wrap it around an injury to soak up the blood and keep the wound clean. Stops bleeding.

COLTSFOOT A flowering plant, a bit like a dandelion, with yellow or white flowers. The leaves can be chewed into a pulp, which is eaten to help shortness of breath.

COMFREY Identifiable by its large leaves and small bell-shaped flowers, which can be pink, white, or purple. The fat black roots of this plant can be chewed into a poultice to mend broken bones or soothe wounds.

DOCK A plant similar to sorrel. The leaf can be chewed up and applied to soothe scratches.

DRIED OAK LEAF Collected in the autumn and stored in a dry place. Stops infections.

FEVERFEW A small bush with flowers like daisies. The leaves can be eaten to cool down body temperature, particularly for cats with fever or chills.

GOLDENROD A tall plant with bright yellow flowers. A poultice of this is terrific for healing wounds.

HONEY A sweet, golden liquid created by bees. Difficult to collect without getting stung, but great for soothing infections or the throats of cats who have breathed smoke.

HORSETAIL A tall plant with bristly stems that grows in marshy areas. The leaves can be used to treat infected wounds. Usually chewed up and applied as a poultice.

JUNIPER BERRIES A bush with spiky dark green leaves and purple berries. The berries soothe bellyaches and help cats who are having trouble breathing.

LAVENDER A small purple flowering plant. Cures fever.

MARIGOLD A bright orange or yellow flower that grows low to the ground. The petals or leaves can be chewed into a pulp and applied as a poultice to wounds. Stops infection.

MOUSE BILE A bad-smelling liquid that is the only remedy for ticks. Dab a little moss soaked in bile on a tick and it'll fall right off. Wash paws thoroughly in running water afterward.

POPPY SEED Small black seeds shaken from a dried poppy flower, these are fed to cats to help them sleep. Soothes cats suffering from shock and distress. Not recommended for nursing queens.

STINGING NETTLE The spiny green seeds can be administered to a cat who's swallowed poison, while the leaves can be applied to a wound to bring down swelling.

TANSY A strong-smelling plant with round yellow flowers. Good for curing coughs, but must be eaten in small doses.

THYME This herb can be eaten to calm anxiety and frayed nerves.

WATERMINT A leafy green plant found in streams or damp earth. Usually chewed into a pulp and then fed to a cat suffering bellyache.

WILD GARLIC Rolling in a patch of wild garlic can help prevent infection, especially for dangerous wounds like rat bites.

YARROW A flowering plant whose leaves can be made into a poultice and applied to wounds or scratches to expel poison.

NOTE:

DEATHBERRIES Red berries that can be fatally poisonous to kits and elders. They are NOT a medicine. Known to Twolegs as yew berries. BEWARE!

CATS OUTSIDE
THE CLANS

BLOODCLAN

Clan character: Not so much a Clan as a loosely organized group of cats who have come together for their mutual protection in hostile and crowded living conditions. These cats have no warrior code, no belief in StarClan, no ceremonies, and no formal training for young cats. Their leader rules by strength and fear.

Habitat: Twolegplace.

Leader: Scourge is a small black cat with icy blue eyes and a high-pitched voice. He wears a collar studded with the teeth of the dogs and cats he has killed, and attached to his claws are dog's teeth. Cruel, calculating, and deadly, Scourge murdered Tigerstar with one blow.

Deputy: Scourge does not have an official deputy, but the closest cat to him is Bone, a large, muscular, black-and-white tom with green eyes. He does all of Scourge's dirty work and reinforces the black cat's leadership with violence and brutality. He also wears a collar studded with teeth.

Notable history: Came to the forest after being offered a deal by Tigerstar, recently made leader of ShadowClan. In return for helping him drive out the other Clans, BloodClan would be allowed hunting rights in the forest. Firestar told Scourge about Tigerstar's past, how he had tried over and over to control the whole forest and failed every time, and how he lied, betrayed, and murdered to satisfy his endless greed for power. Scourge refused to fight on Tigerstar's behalf, and when Tigerstar insisted, Scourge killed him, ripping all nine lives from him with a single blow. With Tigerstar dead, the forest Clans united against BloodClan and drove them out, back to Twolegplace. Scourge himself was killed by Firestar, leader of ThunderClan and Tigerstar's chief opponent.

BARLEY SPEAKS:
Flight from BloodClan

I never questioned my life with BloodClan until I met Fuzz. I thought all cats lived in terror, afraid of being punished by one of Scourge's minions. I thought every cat had to find his food by scrabbling through Twoleg trash. I thought all cats slept in dark, cold alleys and dreaded the day they got too sick or too old to take care of themselves.

My mother taught me and my littermates how to scrounge for food and how to fight. She loved us, but she had to be harsh, or we would never learn to survive. When we were twelve moons old, she threw us out of her den. She had no choice. Scourge had decreed that all cats must fend for themselves. I think he was afraid that strong families might challenge him. As long as we were isolated from one another, we had to rely on Scourge.

I knew my two brothers would seek out Bone and try to become part of Scourge's guard. They admired strength and power, and they wanted some for themselves.

Although it was against the rules, my sister and I stayed together. Violet was a tiny cat, pale orange with thin darker orange stripes. Her paws were small and white and always seemed too delicate for the hard Thunderpaths we ran across or the dirty garbage heaps we had to dig through. We found a hollow below a bush in a Twoleg park where we both could live.

It wasn't a great den. Rain seeped through the branches and into the ground until we were shivering and soaked. And there were always Twolegs around, often with dogs, who sniffed loudly at the entrance to our den.

Violet was terrified of both the Twolegs and the dogs, and I was terrified that Bone would find out we were living together. I convinced her that she should stay inside the den all the time. It was safer, and I could hunt for both of us. I think she was relieved. She could still go out at night, when the park was empty, and stretch her legs in the moonlight.

Bone caught me a few times with an extra mouse in my teeth. When he snarled at me, I would give him both mice and tell him they were an offering for Scourge. He liked that, although he must have known I was lying, just as I knew that those mice would disappear into his own mouth the moment I walked away.

Once I ran into my brothers as they patrolled the dump where Scourge made his den. At first I nearly didn't recognize them. Their eyes were now cold and hard. And around their necks were collars studded with teeth. I stopped and stared at them as they strutted up to me.

"Jumper?" I meowed. "Hoot?"

"Those aren't our names anymore," Hoot sneered. "I am Snake."

"And I am Ice," hissed Jumper. "And don't even think about hunting here."

I hurried away. I'd had my ears battered enough by Scourge's guards. In fact, my ribs were aching and my back leg was bleeding from a beating I had received the morning I met Fuzz. Bone and one of his guards had decided to demonstrate fighting skills on me for a pair of terrified kits.

When I got away, I limped onto a small Thunderpath, looking for prey that lived on the edge of the forest. A Twoleg monster came out of nowhere. I shot up the nearest tree and over a fence so fast that I tumbled off and landed with a thud in the grass.

"*Mrrrow!*" a voice exclaimed. "That was some jump!"

My whole body tensed to run, but I was too winded to scramble back up. I lay there as the strange cat padded closer. I could tell from his scent that he wasn't BloodClan. He smelled of milk and Twolegs. There was the bright blue collar around his neck, with a small silver bell that jingled as he moved. He was plumper than BloodClan cats, and his long gray fur was feathery and well-groomed. He looked at me as if the moon had fallen into his yard.

"My name is Fuzz!" He jumped back into a play-crouch. "What's yours?"

"Er—Barley," I meowed.

"Hello, Erbarley!" Fuzz meowed.

"No, just Barley," I meowed.

"All right, Justbarley," Fuzz meowed.

I began to get the idea that this wasn't the brightest cat I'd ever met.

"You should let my Twolegs take a look at that leg."

"Oh, no!" I couldn't think of anything more alarming.

"Don't worry," Fuzz purred. "They do this all the time. It's their job." He let out a yowl loud enough to wake a sleeping badger on the far side of the forest. The door to the Twoleg nest swung open, and a tree-tall Twoleg male stepped out into the garden.

I must have blacked out. When I awoke, I was nestled in something soft, surrounded by warmth. I opened my eyes slowly.

Fuzz's face was a mouse-length from my own, peering at me with his giant green eyes.

"You're awake!" he meowed, sounding delighted and amazed. "Have some milk!"

I twisted around to sniff at my leg. It was wrapped in a soft white web of stuff and felt much better. I tried to stand and realized I could put my weight on it with only a little pain.

Suddenly I remembered Violet. I glanced up at the window. The sky outside was dark.

"How long have I been here?" I asked Fuzz.

"All day," Fuzz meowed cheerfully.

"I have to get back to my sister," I meowed, scrambling to my feet. "She'll be so worried."

"Well, eat something before you go," Fuzz urged me. I swiped my tongue around the saucer, licking up the scraps of tuna that were left. The flavor was dazzling. Fuzz led me through a flap in the door. Then I was back out in the yard, scrambling over the fence and hurrying back to the park.

The moon was high in the sky when I reached our den.

"Violet?" I called, crawling into the darkness below the branches. "Violet?"

Bone's scent hit my nose just before he spoke from the shadows. "Your sister is not here."

I froze, all my muscles turning to stone. "W-where is she?" I stammered.

"She came looking for you." The black-and-white cat stood and stretched his long, muscular legs. His eyes gleamed in the fragments of moonlight. "What an interesting setup you have here, Barley. You and your sister, living in this den. Isn't that *against the rules?*"

"I'm just taking care of her," I meowed. "We're no threat to Scourge."

"That is for Scourge to decide," Bone hissed. "Come." He stalked out of the bush, brushing past the thorns as if he didn't feel them. I hurried after him, my heart sinking as we approached the trash heap where Scourge held court.

The small black cat was perched atop a mound of discarded Twoleg things. The teeth on his collar and claws glinted like the freezing chips of ice that were his eyes. Cats were gathered all around the mound, waiting for something to happen. Below Scourge, in a cleared circle of dirt, my sister was sitting with her shoulders hunched. Her eyes were huge and terrified.

"Violet," I cried, springing forward, but Bone whirled around and slammed his paw into my head so I was knocked aside, my vision spinning. I crouched for a moment, shaking my head.

"This is what we do with cats who break the rules," Scourge hissed in his eerily high-pitched voice. He flicked his tail at the shadows to his left. My brothers emerged into the moonlight, their teeth bared in furious snarls.

"No!" I yowled. "Leave her alone! Fight me, if you must! She's done no harm!"

"It's true," Scourge snarled. "You are the one who broke the rules. You are the one who must be punished." He swiped his tongue over his paw, making us all wait for a long, horrible moment. Then he looked down at me with a sinister twitch of his whiskers. "And what better punishment could there be than for you to watch your sister die right in front of you."

"No!" I wailed, but before I could move, Bone leaped on me and pinned me down. I could only struggle futilely, my claws scrabbling at the ground, as Snake and Ice stalked up to Violet. There was a flash of claws and a shriek of pain from Violet. And then my poor little sister was lying on the ground, blood spilling out of her, her paws twitching feebly. I stared in horror as Snake and Ice licked the blood off their paws and slunk back into the shadows. Scourge nodded, looking pleased, and then he melted away into the darkness, with all his followers disappearing behind him. Bone lifted his paws and looked down at me with disgust in his eyes.

"Don't ever try to fight BloodClan again," he snarled. "We always win."

Then he too vanished into the darkness.

I crawled over to Violet, my breathing coming in ragged gasps. She was so still, so small. I nosed her face gently and suddenly her eyes opened.

"Barley." She coughed. "Help me."

She was alive! I frantically tried to stop the blood spilling out of the long slice in her stomach, but I didn't know anything about healing another cat.

Then I remembered Fuzz and the Twoleg. It was risky, but it was the only thing I could think of to do.

I closed my mouth gently around the scruff of Violet's neck and dragged her out of the dump. She kept letting out little yips of pain, but she didn't struggle. I dragged her all the way down the small Thunderpath to the gate in the Twoleg fence where Fuzz lived. And then I laid her down on the path and started yowling with all my heart.

Fuzz shot out the cat door a few moments later, his face as

brightly confused as ever. He sprang up to the top of the gate and teetered precariously, gawking at me and Violet.

"Who's *that*?" he exclaimed. "She's the most beautiful cat I've ever seen! Why is she so sad? Oh, my whiskers, is she bleeding too? What on earth is wrong with your Twolegs? Why don't they take better care of you?"

"Fuzz, I need your help," I panted. "I need your Twoleg to take care of Violet for me."

"Where are you going?" Fuzz asked, all wide-eyed innocence. Until he said that, I hadn't really thought about it. I knew I couldn't stay anywhere near BloodClan. She would be safe only here in this Twoleg nest—and she would be safe only if I was far away. Then perhaps Scourge and Bone would forget about us.

"The far side of the forest," I meowed. "Please will you take care of her?"

"Sure," Fuzz meowed. "She doesn't look like she eats much tuna. Maybe she'll share hers with me." He tilted his head at Violet.

The door opened behind him, spilling yellow light into the garden. I bent my head to whisper in Violet's ear.

"You'll be safe now," I meowed. "Remember, I love you."

She blinked up at me. "I love you too, Barley."

"I'll always be your brother," I meowed. "However far apart we are."

"Bye, Justbarley!" Fuzz meowed.

I dashed across the Thunderpath and up a tree. From there, I watched as the Twoleg swung open the gate and saw Violet. He made a sad, shocked sound, then leaned over to gently pick her up. From the way he cradled her as they went back inside, I could tell that he would take care of her. I didn't know why I felt so sure we could trust him, but I did.

Fuzz scampered after them. His long, fluffy tail whisking through the door was the last I saw of the Twoleg nest before I turned and ran swiftly toward the woods.

I traveled quickly through the trees. I could smell other cats around me, but I was afraid they would be like BloodClan, so I didn't stop. I crossed a stream and ran through a clearing guarded by four tall oak trees. I scrambled up a rocky slope and found myself on an open moor, where I ran even faster, as if my life depended on it. I wanted to put as much distance as I could between myself and BloodClan.

Finally, as the sun was rising over the distant hills, I came to a large Twoleg nest. It smelled of hay and mice and sunshine. I could tell after a short exploration that Twolegs came here often but didn't stay long. Something about it felt safe and friendly. Nothing could have been more different from the dark alleys and cold puddles of Twolegplace.

I dug my way into a pile of hay and curled up, breathing in the sweet warmth.

I would be safe here. Safe and free to live my own life. Maybe one day I'd go back and look for Violet—or maybe she'd be happy living with Fuzz and his Twolegs. Maybe she'd get plump on tuna and sleep on the bed with the Twolegs, purring contentedly. The important thing was we'd escaped from BloodClan.

Scourge couldn't hurt us anymore.

THE TRIBE OF RUSHING WATER

Tribe character: Smaller and leaner than forest cats. They smear their fur with mud for camouflage against the rocks. Tribe cats are born as either cave-guards or prey-hunters and are known as *to-bes* while training. Their warrior ancestors belong to the Tribe of Endless Hunting, cats who appear in whispers in the leaves and the pattern of water over stones. Their most sacred place is the Cave of Pointed Stones, where the Healer may interpret signs in the way rain drips from the roof and in the shadows of the stalagmites and stalactites cast by moonlight.

Habitat: The mountains.

Camp: A rocky path leads behind a waterfall into a huge cave, as broad as the waterfall and screened from the outside world by the rushing water. The cave burrows under the mountain. Narrow passages lead off on either side, one to the Cave of the Pointed Stones, one to the nursery. Cats sleep in hollows on the cave floor lined with moss and eagle or heron feathers. A trickle of water runs down a mossy rock into a small, clear pool, providing fresh drinking water.

Leader (known as Healer): Teller of the Pointed Stones, called *Stoneteller*, is a wise old brown tabby cat who serves as both leader and medicine cat. He is responsible for reading the signs in the Cave of Pointed Stones, and he guides his Tribe according to the messages from the Tribe of Endless Hunting.

STONETELLER SPEAKS:
The Coming of the Silver Cat

There are strangers in our cave tonight.

They are returning to their home in the forest, but they must not linger there long. They say that a terrible danger is destroying their home. Soon all the forest cats must go on a journey to no cat knows where. . . .

We are struggling with a terrible danger too. I cannot tell the strangers about it. I fear they would leave the mountains if they knew. And yet one of them must save us from Sharptooth.

I have read the ripple of shadows on the rock wall, the drops of water in the moonlight. I have seen bright gray fur flash in the pool. The signs are clear. A silver cat, not from this Tribe, will come to save us from Sharptooth—that is what the Tribe of Endless Hunting has promised.

The six cats arrived wet and shivering in our cave. They are scrawny, tired, and suspicious, and one of them is badly injured. I have heard them whispering about us—they don't realize how good our hearing is. They can see that we are afraid of something.

I believe the silver cat must be the one called Stormfur. His fur gleams with the dark silver of the moon when it is just a claw in the sky.

The dark tabby, the one called Brambleclaw, is their leader, although the small black cat and the tortoiseshell don't hesitate to challenge him. Nor does the ginger she-cat named Squirrelpaw, yet I can see her respect for him in every ripple of her fur. There is something about those two—a destiny longer, darker, and more fraught with danger than I care to look at. But it does not affect my Tribe.

Once the strangers dried off, I saw there was another silver cat in the group—Stormfur's sister, Feathertail. Could the prophecy refer to her instead? No, it must be Stormfur. He has a proud courage about him, a strength in those shoulders that would defeat any of my cave-guards.

Whatever he is going to do to save us, I hope it will be soon. My Tribe has lost so many cats already. And it is not only the lives of the dead cats that Sharptooth has taken. He has taken the pride, the joy, the fierce will to live of all my Tribe. We are but a shadow of a Tribe now, haunted by the flashing claws and teeth of a mindless killer.

I beseech you, Tribe of Endless Hunting. Guide the silver cat's paws to save us from Sharptooth, so that we may have peace again.

ROGUES AND LONERS

A rogue is a Clan cat who has been banished for crimes against the warrior code. These cats are usually hostile and live as outlaws on Clan territory or on the outskirts. Loners are cats who choose to live neither in Clans nor with Twolegs. They live and hunt alone. Loners can be friendly and even helpful to the Clan cats.

BARLEY: A black-and-white tom who left BloodClan to live as a loner in the forest. (See *Barley Speaks: Flight from BloodClan*.) His home is a warm barn north of WindClan territory. Warriors often pass through his farm on their way to Highstones, and so most of the Clans know of him. The Twolegs who run the farm don't mind him living there, since he keeps down the rodent population.

Barley bravely came to the aid of Bluestar during a rat attack when she was leading four ThunderClan cats back to the forest from Mothermouth. Later, he offered his barn as shelter for WindClan while they journeyed home to their camp. When BloodClan came to the forest, he was able to give Firestar insight into their weaknesses, which helped LionClan win the battle.

RAVENPAW: A small black loner, originally a ThunderClan apprentice. His mentor was the ThunderClan deputy Tigerclaw. During a battle at Sunningrocks, Ravenpaw saw Tigerclaw kill the ThunderClan deputy, Redtail. This knowledge put Ravenpaw's life at risk. With the help of Firepaw, he fled the ThunderClan camp to the safety of Barley's barn. He is happy here; the loner lifestyle suits him better than Clan life.

SASHA: A tawny-colored rogue. She fell in love with Tigerstar while he was recruiting BloodClan. She bore him two kittens, Mothwing and Hawkfrost, and brought them to RiverClan for a better life, as she wasn't interested in raising kits by herself. Later, she tried unsuccessfully to convince them to rejoin her instead of traveling to the Clans' new home.

PURDY: An elderly, mottled brown tabby tom who met the questing Clan cats on their way to the sun-drown-place. Purdy did his best to help the cats find their way through the confusing tangle of Thunderpaths and Twoleg nests, although it might not have been by the shortest route! He tried to warn the young cats of the danger in the mountains, but it was their destiny to go that way, no matter what he said.

SMOKY, DAISY, AND FLOSS: These three cats live as loners in a barn near the horseplace. They do not hunt prey, since they are fed by the Twolegs. This, in the opinion of many Clan cats, makes them as useless as kittypets.

Smoky is a muscular gray-and-white tom, who is distant but not unfriendly. He met the Clan cats on their way to the first Gathering. He is the father of Daisy's kits: Berrykit, Hazelkit, and Mousekit.

Daisy is a creamy brown she-cat with blue eyes. She brought her kits to join ThunderClan.

Floss is a small gray-and-white she-cat, whose kits were taken away by the Nofurs (their name for Twolegs).

DAISY SPEAKS:
My Only Hope

"**Y**our kits! Where have they gone?"

The barn suddenly seemed a large, forbidding space, with a thousand different places for kits to get hurt. I scrabbled through a stack of hay next to my friend Floss. She had recently had kits—but her kits had vanished.

"Their eyes were still closed! They couldn't even walk!"

Floss was lying on her side in a patch of sunshine. She blinked large, sad eyes at me.

"It's the Nofurs," she explained. "They take our kits after they're born. They took my first litter too."

"Why would they do that?"

"Maybe they think three cats in one barn are enough?" Floss meowed. "Maybe there are other barns that need cats."

I curled my tail over my stomach as if I could already protect the little lives inside. I thought there might be three of them, from the way they kicked and wriggled.

"But—you never see them again?" I meowed softly.

"One moment they're here." She lifted a paw and licked it. "The next, they're gone."

I studied her face carefully. I think she was more heartbroken than she was letting on. "Then I'll have to leave," I meowed. "I'll take my kits far away from the Nofurs."

"Where will you go?" Floss asked. "And how will you survive, all on your own with a family of hungry mouths?"

She was right. I wasn't used to being on my own. I wouldn't know how to feed myself or my kits. And I would miss the friendship of Floss and Smoky.

"What about those new cats?" I remembered. "The ones who moved to the lake?"

"Strange creatures. Why not find a nice warm barn to live in?" meowed Floss. "It must be cold and wet out there."

It was true; I hated being cold and wet. But some of those wild cats had looked friendly. There was that white tom who had nodded to me, and the orange leader who had warm green eyes.

Floss narrowed her eyes. "We don't know anything about those cats, except that there are a lot of them," she meowed.

But I was sure they would help me. I could carry my kits there, if I needed to. I knew Smoky wouldn't try to stop me. He had always cared more about Floss than me. Perhaps out there I could find a cat to care about me the way Smoky and Floss care about each other. And he'd take care of my kits too.

I knew there were scary things outside the barn, but I was sure that the wild cats would protect me and my kits, so that I could see them grow up. I knew what I was going to call them too: Mouse, Berry, and Hazel. They're going to be fine, strong cats, and I will be there for every pawstep.

KITTYPETS

Cats that live with Twolegs are called kittypets. They wear collars and are usually timid, soft, and scared of Clan cats. They are fed by their Twolegs, and so have no need to hunt. They have only a vague sense of territory beyond their Twolegs' garden.

SMUDGE: Friendly, plump, and contented black-and-white tom. He lived next door to Firestar, whom he knew as Rusty. He sees none of the appeal of the forest or Clan life.

PRINCESS: Firestar's sister. A light brown tabby with a white chest and white paws. She is intrigued by the forest and gave up her son, Cloudkit, to be raised as a ThunderClan cat. Yet she finds it terrifying too; she could never leave her Twolegs to chase mice in the forest! Cloudkit had some trouble adjusting to the warrior code at first, and he has never believed in StarClan, but he is still a brave, loyal ThunderClan warrior.

CODY: Sweet, plucky, tabby kittypet with blue eyes. Cody ran away from her Twolegs, intending only to have a bit of fun before returning home. She was caught by the construction crew tearing down the forest and thrown into a cage with the wild cats. Here, she befriended Leafpaw, and after they were rescued, Cody went with her to ThunderClan. Although she was willing to help the Clan in their hour of need, the precarious, violent life of the warrior cats was not for her, and she returned to her housefolk. She will never forget her friend Leafpaw.

JACQUES AND SUSAN: Jacques is a huge black-and-white tom with a torn ear. Susan is a small tabby she-cat. They live in a Twoleg nest in ShadowClan's lake territory. Both of them are hostile and dangerous, with no warrior code to guide their actions. When the warrior cats moved into their territory, they showed their displeasure by targeting young or weak cats. ThunderClan helped ShadowClan teach them a lesson.

MILLIE: A light gray tabby she-cat. Millie befriended Graystripe when he was captured by Twolegs. When he decided to leave in search of his Clan, she chose to leave her housefolk and go with him. Although she was raised as a kittypet, Graystripe has trained her to fight, and she is committed to becoming a true ThunderClan warrior.

OTHER ANIMALS

FOXES

Russet-red fur, bushy tails, sharp teeth, and
pointed noses. Look a bit like dogs.
Live in dens, often in sandy ground hidden by
undergrowth.
Live alone or with their cubs.
Mean, suspicious, and hostile, they don't eat cats, but they will
kill for pleasure and not just for prey.
They hunt mostly at night and have a strong and unpleasant
smell.

BADGERS

Large, with short black fur and a white stripe
down their long, pointed muzzles.
Small, beady eyes, powerful shoulders, and
sharp claws.
Live in either caves or sets, which are tunnels
underground, bushes, or tree roots.
Live alone or with their kits and have a very
distinctive smell.
Badgers sometimes prey on young cat kits. Can trample their
victims with enormous paws or deliver a deadly bite.

Have tremendously powerful jaws that make it nearly
  impossible to escape their grip.

Midnight: An exceptional badger at the sun-drown-place. She
  has no hostility for cats. She has a special connection with
  StarClan and can speak both Cat and Fox. It was Midnight
  who passed on the message that the Clans must leave the
  forest.

DOGS

Size varies from that of a kit to a
  pony. Fur can be long or short,
  white, brown, black, gray, or a
  mix. Can have pointy or flat
  noses, droopy or sharp ears.
  Make loud, angry noises and
  love chasing cats.

Live mostly in Twoleg nests or barns.
  Wild dogs might sleep anywhere; one pack in recent Clan
  history made their home in the caves below Snakerocks.

Loud, fast, and sharp-toothed. Many dogs seem to be devoted
  to their Twolegs and are seen only in Twoleg company.
  There is a theory that most dogs are too dim-witted to be
  truly dangerous. Packs of dogs are always to be feared. (See
  *ThunderClan, Brightheart Speaks: The Death of
  Swiftpaw.*)

BIRDS OF PREY

Winged predators with hooked beaks and sharp, curving talons, these include hawks, eagles, falcons, and owls.

Nest in hollows or branches of trees, or on the ledges of cliffs.

Extremely sharp vision for spotting prey from a distance. Hawks and eagles are daytime hunters; owls hunt at night. They swoop down from the sky to carry off prey, which includes kits. This was the fate of Snowkit, Speckletail's deaf son, when a hawk attacked the camp after a forest fire had burned away its protective cover. The Tribe of Rushing Water have developed clever ways to hunt these birds.

HORSES/SHEEP/COWS

Four-legged farm creatures.

Horses are tall and swift with flowing manes and tails and giant, pounding hooves.

Sheep look like fluffy white clouds dotted across a green field.

Cows can be black and white or brown, and their hooves are to be avoided.

Large fenced fields and sometimes hay-filled Twoleg barns.

Mostly harmless. However, take caution passing through their fields. A galloping horse or stampeding herd of cows would trample a cat without even noticing.

RATS

Brown-furred and beady-eyed rodents, with long, naked tails
and sharp front teeth. Not much bigger than kits.

Live in garbage dumps like Carrionplace in ShadowClan
territory or anywhere they can scavenge Twoleg food.

Live and travel in packs. Individually they pose no threat to
cats, but their numbers are often overwhelming, and bites
can cause infection. A single rat contaminated the whole of
ShadowClan during Nightstar's brief time as leader.

TWOLEGS

Tall, smooth-skinned creatures with some fur on their heads.
Walk on two legs.

Live in large, boxy nests with hard roofs and floors, often
surrounded by tidy gardens and fences.

Also known as Nofurs or Upwalkers. Twolegs ride around in
monsters and seem to like dogs. They are to be avoided if
possible, as they are capable of doing something
unpredictable at any moment, such as tearing down a tree,
starting a fire, or locking up a cat for no reason.

MYTHOLOGY

Every Clan has its legends—the great adventures
of its warrior ancestors, passed down through the generations.
But all the Clans share the stories of the ancient, giant, gold-pelted
cats who once ruled the forest. LionClan had flowing manes,
like the rays of the sun. LeopardClan were swift; they had black spots
on their pelts like racing pawprints. TigerClan were flame-
colored night hunters, with black stripes like shadows flickering
across their fur and the darkness of night in their souls. The giant cats
are gone now, but they have passed down special talents to their
descendants, the warrior cats.

HOW LEOPARDCLAN WON THE RIVER

In a time when the forest was young and untouched by Twolegs, the three Clans of mighty cats came together for a Gathering during the frosts of leaf-bare.

The leader of LionClan, a proud cat named Goldenstar, stepped forward.

"There is a wild boar loose in the forest," he roared.

"There are many wild boar loose in the forest," responded Swiftstar, the LeopardClan leader, with a dismissive flick of his tail.

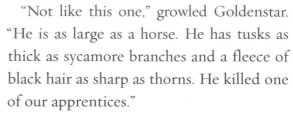

"Not like this one," growled Goldenstar. "He is as large as a horse. He has tusks as thick as sycamore branches and a fleece of black hair as sharp as thorns. He killed one of our apprentices."

"I know of this boar too," rumbled the TigerClan leader, Shadestar, twitching her ears. "We call him Rage. A TigerClan hunting party met him in the woods two days ago, but he escaped us. He fights with the strength of ten warriors and can kill with a single blow of his fierce tusks."

"Ha!" A voice rose from the crowd of warriors, which parted to reveal a LeopardClan warrior named Fleetfoot. "Such a beast would be no match for a LeopardClan warrior," she boasted. "We would outrun it, outsmart it, and kill it."

"Oh, yes?" Shadestar snarled. "Then why don't you do as you say and kill Rage?"

"Show us that your deeds can match your words," growled Goldenstar.

"With pleasure," Fleetfoot responded proudly.

"And in exchange," Swiftstar quickly added, "LeopardClan may claim the river as our hunting grounds."

"Hmm," meowed Shadestar, narrowing her eyes.

"Very well," Goldenstar agreed. "If Fleetfoot kills this beast, LeopardClan may claim the river for one moon, during which no other Clan will hunt there."

Swiftstar bowed his head in agreement. He leaped down from the Great Rock and swept out of the clearing, with his LeopardClan warriors pouring after him.

Shadestar turned to Goldenstar as the spotted cats disappeared from sight. "There is something we didn't tell Fleetfoot."

"I know," meowed Goldenstar. "She will find it out soon

enough. Rest assured, we will not have to give up the river and its hunting grounds."

The hunt began that night. Fleetfoot tracked the boar by its scent until she found him under a tall oak tree, nosing the ground underneath it. She leaped at him with a ferocious yowl, and the boar, startled, turned and ran. Fleetfoot chased Rage through the forest, leaping fallen trees, dodging bushes, staying close on his heels.

At last they burst out into an open patch of ground, and before the boar could stop himself, he went hurtling off a cliff. Fleetfoot leaped after him into the torrent of the river below. She found him thrashing around and wrapped her claws around his back, pinning him under the water until she thought she would burst for want of air.

As the sun rose over the gorge, Fleetfoot and Rage washed up on the shore of the river. The wild boar was dead.

Fleetfoot staggered to her feet, dripping wet and trying to catch her breath. Then she saw something that made her fur prickle all along her spine. Standing on the bank of the river was the boar's mate—an even bigger, fiercer beast who rarely left her den, as Goldenstar and Shadestar knew. This she-boar was named Fury.

Fleetfoot and Fury fought on the bank of the river for two nights and two days. Finally, exhausted, Fleetfoot drove the she-boar out onto the stepping-stones, where Fury lost her footing, fell into the river, and drowned.

Goldenstar and Shadestar were ashamed of their treachery. The young LeopardClan warrior had saved them all from two terrible enemies. So, they gave LeopardClan sole hunting rights to the river forever.

And that is how LeopardClan won the river.

HOW SNAKES CAME TO THE FOREST

There once lived a brave LionClan warrior called Sunpelt. Sunpelt had heard stories of the giant snake called Mouthclaw, who lived in a dark cave by Snakerocks. She was the only snake in the entire forest. She had killed many great warriors from all the Clans. Her sharp-fanged jaws could swallow a living cat whole, and she spat deadly venom.

Cats from all Clans were forbidden to go to Snakerocks. The leaders were afraid to lose any more warriors to Mouthclaw. But Sunpelt wanted to prove what a great warrior he was. He thought that by killing Mouthclaw, he would earn the respect of the forest.

One morning he left the camp before sunup and journeyed to Snakerocks. He stood outside Mouthclaw's cave and called, "Come out and fight!" Then he angered her further by kicking stones into her cave with his back legs.

Mouthclaw slithered out of her cave, her tongue flickering like lightning. She was ten fox-lengths long and as thick as a badger with a bellyful of cubs. Her eyes were evil red slits, and her scales glittered in the dawn light.

She bared her fangs with pleasure, for LionClan warriors were one of her favorite meals. And then she lunged. But the young warrior was too quick. He leaped from rock to rock, while Mouthclaw spat poison and threw up clouds of dust with her lashing tail. The fight went on all day, but she could never get close enough for the kill.

Finally Mouthclaw could fight no more.

"I have been living in these rocks for a thousand m
hissed. "Spare my life, and I shall grant you one wish."

The brave warrior thought for a moment. Then he roared, "I
wish that you would shrink to the length of a cat's tail. If you were
that small, then I would allow you to remain living at Snakerocks."

"And that is all you ask of me?" hissed Mouthclaw with an evil
glint in her eyes.

"That is all," said Sunpelt. He knew a tiny snake would be no
danger to the giant cats of the forest. He would be a hero.

Mouthclaw began to writhe and slither, back and forth. A great
cloud of dust rose up, and when it settled, Sunpelt leaped back-
ward in horror.

A thousand snakes, each the length of a cat's tail, covered the
ground, spitting poison. Now instead of one giant snake at
Snakerocks, there were many, each of them deadly and fierce.

Sunpelt could not believe what he had done. Horrified and
guilt-stricken, he raced back to camp and confessed all to his
leader.

At first Goldenstar was angry. "This was a dangerous thing you
did," he growled. "You should know better than to bargain with
snakes. They are cunning and will outwit us every time."

"I know," Sunpelt admitted, hanging his head.

"However," Goldenstar meowed, "you have done a great service for the forest. These smaller snakes may be dangerous, but
none can be as dangerous as Mouthclaw. Now no warrior has to
fear being swallowed or bitten by her deadly fangs."

"That is true," Sunpelt meowed, his spirit rising.

Goldenstar forgave his brave warrior. After all, Sunpelt was not
the first cat—or the last—to be tricked by a snake in the grass.

HOW TIGERCLAN GOT THEIR STRIPES

When the big cats first walked the forest, TigerClan and LionClan both had pure gold coats, but only LionClan cats had a mane of long hair like the rays of the sun. The TigerClan cats were jealous of these golden manes, and they were jealous of LeopardClan's ability to run faster than any other cats. Jealousy made them bitter, and they started hunting at night and keeping to the shadows during the daytime.

One TigerClan warrior, Thorntooth, was more bitter than the rest. He started attacking the other Clans at night, stealing their kits and raiding their fresh-kill pile. Shadestar, the TigerClan leader, knew what Thorntooth was doing, but she did nothing to stop him, because her own heart was black with envy.

Then a day came when Thorntooth sneaked back to camp with a small lion cub dangling from his jaws and mewling sadly.

Shadestar took one look at the kit and flew into a rage.

"That's Petalkit!" she roared. "You've stolen Goldenstar's only daughter!"

"Yes, I have," Thorntooth replied smugly, dropping the she-cat on the ground. Petalkit let out a wail and buried her nose in her paws.

"What have you done?" Shadestar snarled. "This will mean war. LionClan will not rest until they rescue this kit. They will slaughter us all if they have to."

"We can fight them," Thorntooth growled angrily.

"And let TigerClan warriors die? For what?" Shadestar hissed. "For nothing. We are giving Goldenstar's daughter back immediately."

Shadestar called a Gathering that night and gave Petalkit back to Goldenstar before LionClan could attack. Here was proof that Thorntooth was behind the night raids. Goldenstar and Swiftstar demanded that Shadestar put a stop to her warrior's dishonorable behavior.

"But it's not fair!" Thorntooth protested. "TigerClan has nothing special. We are plain orange cats with no great skills. We should have something to set us apart like LionClan and LeopardClan have!"

"Enough!" Goldenstar snarled. "Shadestar, your Clan must be punished. For the next moon, TigerClan shall not be seen in daylight. The light of the sun shall not touch your pelts. You may not speak to cats of other Clans. For one whole moon, you forfeit your Clan's honor. If you stop your raids, you may rejoin the Clans at the next Gathering."

So TigerClan walked only by night for a moon and stayed away from the other Clans. When the full moon came around again, they stepped into the Gathering under the moonlight. All the other cats gasped.

"Your pelts!" Swiftstar meowed.

TigerClan had spent so long walking in the shadows that their brightly colored pelts were sliced through with jet-black stripes. Thorntooth was pleased, because now TigerClan was marked out like the other Clans.

From that day on, all TigerClan cats were born with stripes.

GLOSSARY

Catspeak: Humanspeak

Crow-food: rotting food

Fox dung: an insult; stronger offense than mouse-brain

Fresh-kill: recently killed prey

Gathering: a meeting that the Clans hold in peace at every full moon

Greencough: severe chest infection, which can be fatal in elders and young kits

Greenleaf: summer

Greenleaf Twolegplace: a place where humans visit only in the summer (a campsite, resort, etc.)

Halfbridge: a dock

Horseplace: fields and stables near the lake where half-tamed cats live

Housefolk: a house cat's word for its humans

Kittypet: a house cat

Leaf-bare: winter

Leaf-fall: fall/autumn

Loner: cat that lives peacefully on its own in one place but doesn't defend its territory

Monster: usually refers to human machines such as cars and bulldozers

Moonhigh: the time of night when the moon is at its highest—often midnight

Mouse-brained: not very smart

Mouse dung: an insult; stronger than mouse-brain, but less offensive than fox dung

Newleaf: spring

Nofurs: another word for humans

One moon: one month (half-moon = two weeks, quarter-moon = one week)

Rogue: a potentially hostile cat who lives outside the Clans and never spends too long in one place

Sharing tongues: term used to describe cats grooming each other

Silverpelt: the Milky Way

Sun-drown-place: the sea to the west, where the sun sets

Sunhigh: noon

Thunderpath: a road

Tree-eater: bulldozer

Twoleg nest: a human house

Twolegplace: a human town

Twolegs: the Clans' word for humans

Upwalkers: another word for humans

Whitecough: mild chest infection

Property of (no surprise)

MOONZ
BALLOONZ